Bay Tree Books
presents
Sapling Short Stories 2005

First edition published 2005

Text © 2005 individual authors
Illustrations © 2005 individual illustrators
This edition © 2005 Bay Tree Books Ltd

The moral rights of the author and illustrator
have been asserted

ISBN 0-9551377-0-5

Published by Bay Tree Books Ltd,
96 High Street West, Glossop, Derbyshire SK13 8BB

A catalogue record for this book is available
from the British Library

Preface

Several months ago, we ran a short story competition for local children of all school ages. We received an overwhelming response and published authors, Liz, Helen and David, then had the unenviable task of judging the entries.

This is a selection of one hundred and one of those stories, but we should congratulate every child who entered the competition for their incredible effort and wonderful imaginations.

We hope you enjoy reading them as much as we have.

Sarah and Sarah

PS. As these stories are written by children, we accept that there may be some elements of plagiarism! Hopefully the original authors will be flattered that they provided inspiration.

Contents

I Went To A Farm
by Francesca Castillo aged 6

One day I went to a farm with my dad. When we got there we looked around and there were animals everywhere. First we went to the lambs and sheep. I fed one of the lambs. After that I asked my dad if I could have the lamb and dad asked the farmer and he said yes! So we took him home. The first day the lamb was fine. The second day he pooed on the carpet. The third day he weed on my mum, dad and brother. The fourth day he was very naughty. The next day we took him back and we never had any fuss again.

The Patchwork Dog
by Ella Nixon aged 6

In a far, far away land there lived a patchwork dog. The patchwork dog lived next to a wicked bat kind of thing with razor sharp teeth and giant wings as brown as can be. He wanted to catch the patchwork dog whose name is Patch. Patch lived on the coastline with his mum. One day his mum said, "I have to go somewhere." "Can I come?" woofed Patch. "Sorry Patch, you can't come," whined his mother. Patch thought oh no! I will be left with b b Brown bat. Brown was his name. Just then he heard a knock at the door. Patch opened the door. It was Brown. "Goodbye Mrs Dance," hissed Brown. For two hours they stared at each other. Then Brown said, "Tea time." Patch barked, "What is for tea?" He answered

"A dog called Patch and some peas, yummy hey Patch!" "N-n-n-not really B-b-b-brown." But before Brown could open the oven door Patch's mum came, Patch growled, "What's for dinner mama?" "Planned it already sweetie. Fresh bat and peas and bat blood to drink, I have got some bat cream as well for pudding." "Sounds yummy mama." They really enjoyed the dinner and that was the end of bat.

Off To The Moon
by Nathan Jackson-Turner aged 6

One day me and my dad got on a plane. We fastened our belts and we went up so fast that I thought I was dizzy. And it was getting dark and a voice said, "Welcome into space." We crashed into the moon! So we got out and we saw a moon monster. But he was deadly so we all pulled the plane out of the moon and we flew back home.

The Cat That Lost His Spots
by Finn Bridges and Victoria Greensmith aged 8

How could a poor kitty tumble in the washer?
Spots, a pretty five-month-old kitten, had a lucky escape last Monday lunchtime when his owner put him in the washing. Last Monday, Jenny, Spots' new owner, bought him a ball from the shops in Hayfield where they live. When they got home Jenny left Spots alone to play. The new ball rolled away and Spots ran after it.

the ball rolled into the basket of dirty
was very big. Spots dived in and started
Later, Jenny put the washing in the
washing machine with Spots still looking for the ball; in
he went with the dirty washing. Jenny walked out of the
room to get a drink. Little did she know that Spots was
whirling in the washing machine with the washing. His
spots gradually peeled off. Soon Jenny heard a scraping
noise on the glass. Quickly she opened the door and
water went everywhere. The stuttering cat coughed and
fell over. Jenny had this to say, "I never meant to put
him in the wash but now he can't walk in a straight line
and he is coughing up bubbles!"

The Scientist And The Prince
by Isabel Raban aged 6

Once upon a time there was a baddy scientist and a
goody prince who hated each other. The scientist lived
in a spooky house and the prince lived in a beautiful
tower. They met each other and pretended to be friends
but really they hated each other. The scientist invited
the prince to his spooky house with potions and lotions.
The prince did the same and invited him to his palace
where there were lots of guards and traps. The scientist
went. When he got there, the palace was shining like a
piece of gold. Then he got trapped and the guard
looked after him. The prince told him if he said sorry
he could come out, but the scientist didn't say sorry.

The Servant Elves
by Joanna Brown aged 6

Once upon a time there was a family of house elves. House elf means servant in the wizard world and these elves belonged to a school called Hogwarts and they worked in the kitchen. They were trapped there until they were presented with clothes. They helped each other when they needed it. They even helped students and teachers. Once they were set free they burst into tears. They clung to the walls of the kitchen but they were thrown out of the window. They travelled day and night but nobody wanted them. At last they were given another job at Hogwarts.

James The Bully
by Tilly Rostron aged 7

Amy goes to school. She loves school. Apart from James the bully. Everyday he bullies her. She never tells her mum in case she causes trouble. But she tells her best friend Kate. Kate says she should stand up to him. In the morning James asked for her lunch. She tried to stand up to him. But she was just not ready yet. The next day James asked for her collection of marbles. And he got her marbles. They planned to trick him on the bus the next day. It was morning when James got on the bus, Amy scared him by saying BOO!!! The next day James didn't go to school and she lived happily ever after.

A Disaster At Sea
by Jemima Higgins aged 7

One dreamy night a ship came along and waves were splashing along onto the boat. Suddenly, Joseph who was on the boat fell out. Tim found a rope and he said, "Hold onto this rope Joseph." But it was too late, his best friend Joseph drowned. Tim came to an island. He went off the boat and shouted, "Joseph check this erm…erm… island out," as if he thought it was a dream. But it wasn't, it was true. So he looked back on the boat but he wasn't there. Then he went back on the island and saw a lobster. He began to get hungry so he killed the lobster and ate it. Then he began to get tired so he sat next to a palm tree and went to sleep. As he was asleep, monkeys came and pulled Tim's ears and his hair. Then a gold ship came when he was asleep and when he heard someone say, "A-hoy there!" he woke up. Then he saw a pirate and he remembered his dad was a pirate. He said, "Dad?" "Yes my son, where is Joseph?" "Oh him… err… err… he drowned at the bottom of the water. I found a rope but it was too short and too late so he drowned," said Tim. "Don't worry because is this Joseph?" said Tim's dad, "Come on you two, would you help me find some treasure." So they dug and dug for hours and hours and they found some treasure, then they saw a bottle. Then dad the pirate said, "Please can you get that bottle with that piece of paper guys?" So they went into the sea and got the bottle out of the sea. They got the letter out and read the note, it said: Whoever gets this letter, could you rescue me from my house, it is on fire. So they got back on the boat with the note and went to the house on fire. There was a lady who owned the house. The lady had a bucket of water in her hand. She tipped the bucket of water on the fire. Then she turned round and said, "Hello, what's your name?" she asked them. "My name is Tim, this is Joseph and that's my dad, Ben. What's your name?" said Tim. "My name is Sally. Well we're not in a club called name club," said the lady. "We are here to rescue you," said Joseph. "Of course you are," said the lady. "Come with us," said the pirate. "Okay," said the lady. So they got back on the boat and went back to the island. And they spotted a monkey on the island and Tim picked it up and put it back in one of the palm trees. Then they lived on that little island until they died.

The Girl Who Became Famous
by Voirrey Baker aged 7

A long time ago there lived a girl called Francesca. She was eight years old and quite poor. She wanted to make history. One day she was very excited because in the newspaper there was a competition to see if anyone could make history, so she entered it. The next day when she was going to the shops she met a boy. The boy asked her what her name was and she replied

"Francesca," and he squeaked "Simon." Simon asked Francesca if she was in the make history competition and Francesca replied, "Yes," and off she went to get a boy wig and three jobs. Meanwhile, Simon was preparing a giant picnic. The following week she met Simon again. Before the big picnic she tricked him into telling her that he would be making her ill by the picnic. Francesca gave him some alcohol so when it was the competition day everyone else looked silly. She was a footballer, ice-hockey player and soldier! Everyone cheered! She had made history! She lived happily ever after.

The Dragon And The King
by Ben Karnon aged 4

The dragon came to the castle and breathed fire at the king. The king hid in the dungeons. The dragon ate the king.

A Disaster At Sea
by Ella Wragg aged 7

One dark night, a princess was asleep and a giant lobster came through the window and took the sleeping princess. Early in the morning her father woke up (he is a Duke) and peeped in the princess's room. "Aaaahhh," said the Duke, "my daughter is gone!" "Completely gone sir," said one of the maids. Meanwhile, the princess was stranded on an island crying, "Oh dear, oh dear." Then suddenly the princess had an idea. "I know, I can put a letter in a bottle." She had a piece of paper and a pen and wrote a note and put it in the bottle and threw it in the sea. She waited but a pirate picked it up and read it! The pirate had heard about the island and he sailed to it! But the Duke was hiding and he jumped out of the boat, got the princess and jumped into his boat and they went home and lived happily ever after.

Conner And The Alien
by Taylor Wilson aged 5

One sunny day Conner went on his bicycle. He met an alien. He had green pointed ears and brown eyes. He was green all over. The pedal had broken off the rocket, so the alien asked Conner if he could borrow his pedal. Conner said yes he could. When the rocket was fixed they went to the beach. When they were at the beach Conner felt hungry. Conner said, "Lets go and get an ice-cream." When they had eaten the ice cream, Conner felt tired. The alien took him home.

Paradise Park
by Caity Heath aged 6

One sunny day the people were at Paradise Park. Some were playing football. Some were selling ice cream to people. I was running along with my owner. My owner was flying a kite. I am a dog you see. I was running with it. I have brown spots and white fur with a brown nose. My owner had a kite that was brown and yellow. After flying the kite we went home for lunch. After lunch we went back again but my legs were tired so I had a little rest. When I woke up nobody was there, not even my family. I got up, ran back, but I got lost in SINKING SAND! I was half way down now. My head was in it. I swigged and swogged and finally got out. I ran and ran up a tree and then I got down. I got sight of my house. I quickly went in. My family were overjoyed and they had a little party!

The Little Racoon's Brilliant Idea
by Emma Shaw aged 7

Once upon a time there lived a family of racoons. They lived by the water hole in the forest. There was a mum, a dad and a little boy racoon called Robert. One lovely day they were drinking some water at the water hole. Suddenly, a big shadow came up behind them. It looked like some sort of house. It wasn't a house, it was a tent. A tourist came to look at nature. Robert was scared and ran home. But the others weren't scared, they showed him round their home. Robert made friends with the tourist. When it was time to go, the racoons gave the tourist a few things that they didn't need anymore. He put them in the car but the car wouldn't go. What would they do? Robert had a good idea. He could ride on a snake and he did!

Pixie
by Eleanor Robinson aged 5

Once upon a time in a house with a sack he went out in his garden. He found a star. He went back in his mushroom. He played with the star, his star it was magic. The magic star made him grow. He grew to the same size as the children outside. He went to play until he started to go small. Then he ran back home.

The Bears And The Knights
by Finlay Peacock aged 6

Once upon a time there lived a whole army of bears and a whole army of knights. The bears lived in a cave and the knights lived in a castle guarded by archers and pike men. They fight against each other. The pike men killed twelve bears and the other bears killed the archers and pike men. They smashed through the gatehouse and smashed the castle. They were history. The bears won. The bears worked together and smashed down the castle with their animal friends, deer, bunnies and eagles.

The Ghost Train
by Tim Winter aged 5

A long time ago there was a ghost train with a ghost. The ghost was reading a book. The next day he decided to go for a ride on the ghost train. "It is a nice day," said the ghost and he went away. Some bats screamed at him but he didn't mind a bit.

One Icy New Year's Eve
by Jack Heath aged 6

Once upon a time in a small house far, far, far, far away in the country there was a house. In the house there lived a pixie. His name was Peter Pixie. One dark Christmas night, Peter Pixie was ice-skating on a pond. The pond began to crack. Crack, crash, bang, bash, SPLASH. The whole pond cracked. Peter Pixie fell in. He went down and down and down. He decided to swim to shore. He saw a fish. The fish picked Peter up and lifted him to the surface. Peter walked along the path he did not know, so he went one way, which was unfortunately the wrong way.

The Snowman
by Matthew Sonczak aged 6

I made a snowman. He made a snow motorbike. He rode on it. I threw snowballs at him and he fell off. I threw him off a cliff. There was a piece of jelly. He bounced back up. I moved the jelly and threw him off again. He went splat and that was the end of him.

Princess Lucy's Adventure
by Victoria Lovell aged 5

Once upon a time there was a sweet princess called Lucy. She was a beautiful girl and she stayed with her mummy and daddy. She liked to play with Barbies. She had an adventure in the enchanted forest and she climbed up the

Far Away Tree. She went to see the Saucepan Man. She saw the Saucepan Man dancing. She screamed because the Saucepan Man saw her and grabbed her. He put her in a box and sended her to clean his house up. She was very sad. She wished she never went up that Far Away Tree. One of the king's knights saw her up in the Saucepan Man's house. He bringed her back to the King and Queen, and the King and Queen welcomed her back.

A Very Scary Haunted House
by Saul Gillen aged 6

Once upon a time there lived a very happy family. They were going to move house. But every house they bought was wrong. But they found a house. When they got in they all went to bed. In the morning the dad got scared. So they went back home. When they got home they went to bed.

Mole Goes To The Jungle
by Amy Brooks aged 6

Once there was a mole and he lived under ground. One day he was going to the jungle. When he was there he heard a noise, it was a trembling noise. Right in front of mole was a big cave man.

"I'm going to eat you," said the cave man.

"No, don't eat me," said the mole.

And the cave man began to run after little mole. Luckily little mole had some sellotape in his back pack. Little Mole sellotaped the cave man to the tree and told

all the animals to nibble the cave man's clothes.
Luckily mole got home in time for tea.
"When I go to the jungle again, I'll make sure that I'll
go to the one in Africa," he said while he made the tea.

The Fox
by Sam Huyton aged 7

One day, I went downstairs and under our floorboards. I found a fox under the floorboards. It had a broken leg. I helped the fox. We took it to the vets. I put it back under the floorboards. It was called Sam. It ran away. I ran after it. It got stuck in the barbwire. I found the fox. It had broken its leg. It had to have stitches.

Jill And The Mystery Of The Stolen Properties
by Alice Woolley aged 7

Far, far away, where no one has been before, there lived a beautiful rich girl called Jill. She was a detective. One day, Jill was told to capture a robber that was stealing museums' properties. The next day she went on her mission to catch the baddie whose name was Robber Skuse. Jill got a train to Manchester and it stopped at the museum where Robber Skuse was hiding. Robber Skuse knew she was here so he set up a trap. Then Jill came walking by and fell into the trap! When she looked up she saw Robber Skuse. She remembered she had a rope, she threw the rope on a painting and she climbed out. After that... Jill threw another rope at Robber Skuse and wrapped the rope around him and tied it in a tight knot. Suddenly the police cars came! Jill threw Robber Skuse into the police car and that taught him a lesson!

Pirate Pete
by Beth Crane aged 7

Once upon a time there was a pirate. He was called Pete. He was very fat and was bald and had a wooden leg. He was building a house. And he was singing, "A Pirates Life For Me." He was a very jolly man. He had always wanted to find treasure. He wanted to go on a ship. So he went to the garage and painted his car into a ship and he loved it. He painted the road for water and painted treasure on the road. Then he ran around in a circle. He jumped up and down in joy. He went off to look for a toy treasure box. The next day he found a key. "It must be magic," said Pete. So he rubbed it and he went to a place that sold ships. So he bought one and he sailed to an island. It had a cross on it and he wondered what it was for. So he dug it up. He found golden treasure!! But there was a sea creature with a crocodile head and a shark body and he was watching him. But then he saw the baddie. The baddie said, "Wow, that looks heavy, do you want me to carry that for you?" "Ok," said Pete. The baddie took it and ran away. But just then someone found the baddie and killed him. Pete said, "Who are you?" He answered, "Your secret member."

The Cat And The Baddie
by Chloe Morgan aged 6

Once upon a time there lived a goodie and a baddie. One day the baddie went sledging. The goodie saw him and pushed him into the water and the ice split and the baddie nearly got caught by a shark. Then a cat said, "What's all the fuss about?" So the baddie tricked the cat, but the cat was clever and he hadn't been tricked because he had some chocolate with poison in, but the baddie sniffed it and did not eat it. The cat disguised himself so the baddie could not trick him and he locked the door. In the morning the cat went down to the lake to see the shark. It was ill so the shark stayed under water. So the cat went to see her auntie because she was hungry. Her auntie was out so she asked her uncle. Her aunt came home and they went to the theme park and lived happily ever after.

Diamond's Adventure
by Faye Gallagher aged 6

Once upon a time there lived a fish. The fish looked rainbow coloured and had scales like diamonds. Her name was Diamond. There was a man who was evil. His name was Scary, he always used to try and catch Diamond. Diamond lived under the sea and Scary lived in a haunted house. Usually Scary never catches Diamond. But today he did. He went diving under the sea. He dressed up as Sparkle, her friend. He said,

"Hey let's go for a boat trip," and Diamond said, "Ok."
Then Scary took off his costume. "Ha ha ha," said
Scary, "now I've got you." Diamond shouted, "Help,
help! Shark, eat Scary please!" and that was the end of
Scary!

Princess Petronella
by Sophie Langton aged 8

We came to the door with Princess Petronella. The
guards were on our tail. I opened the door, Petronella
fell out down the high rocky snow covered mountains of
Doom! "Oh no," I cried, "what now?" Then we turned
round and the guards were right behind us. "1, 2, 3 run,"
whispered Braveheart, so we did. Soon a blizzard
started and the guards turned round and said, "I give
up." "Phew," I said. We ran down and soon we were at
the river. Then the mountains gave a great rrooo-aaarr
and about 70 kilos of snow fell down. It looked like the
biggest herd of white horses. I felt like a pot of ice-
cream in a freezer. We sheltered by a rock. "Now
what?" asked Braveheart when the earthquake ended.
Lots of snow had fallen on the river. Midge was not
very clever. "Let's just walk along the river, thank you
snow," he shouted up to the mountains. Without
thinking, Midge walked across the river. "Agghh," he
screamed as he fell under the snow. We have to go after
him, so we held our noses and jumped! Then, as we
were swimming we saw Petronella. Soon she saw us

and pushed a tree that had snapped from the earthquake and pushed it into the river. Thanks to Petronella we all grabbed the tree and pulled our bodies across the tree trunk.

It was very scary in the forest of fear, all the trees were hooting down on us. We could hardly see, it was dark and a forbidden Midge was messing with the dragon trap. Then chop, chop, "Agghh," went Midge. The elves jumped out on Midge and pulled Midge to the ground. We jumped on the elves and rescued Midge from the trap by confusing the elves. The elves were just pretending, then they started to run after us shouting, "Come back," in scary voices. Midge raced ahead, then we heard him scream again. We went to see what was the matter. Midge had fallen in the swamp. "Oh no," we said. Just as it couldn't get any worse, a dragon appeared from behind the trees. He had a massive orange horn on his purple plum head, his body was purple too and it was covered in green spots. On his plum head there were two beady, black eyes, two magnificent yellow wings were placed on his scaly back. "I searched far and wide to find this forest of fear," he roared, flapping his wings like a butterfly stuck in a spider web.

"Climb aboard," he boomed. I stepped forward. "No," I said firmly. The dragon looked hurt. "Come on, what do we have to lose?" I stood my ground. "Our lives," I answered. Little John picked me up and put me on the dragon's back. Then he started to beat his wings and we were off home, over forests and rivers, fields of sunflowers and snow topped mountains, towns and villages, and then they all drifted away and so did I. The journey was so long that we all drifted off to a world far away. About an hour later, there was a big crash as they landed and all awoke with a start. "Hurray," they shouted. Braveheart suddenly thought of mum and then he walked in the house and saw it was a surprise party.

Animal Adventure
by Abbie Stokes aged 7

All the animals were glad that they were safe, but they did not know what was ahead of them. It was turning dark, there was howling and whistling trees. A pack of wolves are coming. The animals ran and ran until they came to an old house and there was a hole in the door. They went inside. "Eek eek!" something was there, then there was a rattle. "It's a mouse," said squirrel. "No I'm not," said the mouse, "I'm a vole." "Hey," said one of the other voles, "that's where my nephew got to." "Oh well nephew," said one of the voles, "let's get out of here before the wolves come." So they went and ran, walked and sneaked. It was turning morning again, everyone was asleep, then the rabbit woke up by a loud noise, it was bulldozers. He woke everybody up and said, "Quickly get up, bulldozers are coming." They all got up and ran until nothing was there and the wolves were coming. So they ran straight for the bulldozers, they went around them and kept running and running. The wolves got stuck behind with the bulldozers. They got home and luckily their home wasn't destroyed like everything else.

The animals were glad that their home wasn't destroyed yet, but they didn't know what would happen to their home in the future. So they went to look for food and think what might happen to the home. "Maybe the bulldozers will come back," said squirrel. "Or maybe get washed away in a flood," said hedgehog. Hedgehog was right because it started to rain and the nearest river overflowed, so when the animals got home it was destroyed. So they walked in the rain for miles and miles to find a home, but everything was destroyed and they decided to get out of the woods and have a home somewhere else. So they went out of the woods through a farm where a cat tried to chase them and then came to a river. They tried to cross it but a crocodile snapped the rabbit's tail. "Ow," said the rabbit, "that hurt," and he ran onto the shore. They finally arrived at a new home on a hill where they could see for miles and miles and now they can see the danger heading towards them. Problem solved – almost.

Beth And The Magic Key
by Olivia Claire Marsden aged 7

There was once a girl called Beth. She lived with her family in a little cottage. She was nine years old. She had long blonde hair and lots of friends. She was tall, friendly and young. Her mum and dad were very poor. So they told her to go to a little island with treasure. So she packed her bag and went. When she got there in a little sailboat she said, "This is a very small island." She started digging but she didn't dig very deep until she was asleep. When she was asleep, a mean old witch came and dug the treasure up with a shovel. She didn't take it though. The next day Beth woke up and saw that somebody had dug up the treasure. She wanted to know who it was. She then saw a cave. She went to see what was in it. There was a lady that was really the witch. The lady said, "I have got lots of sweets, if you follow me I will give you some." So Beth followed the witch with her treasure and they went to a little kitchen. The witch said, "Go into that cage and get some sweets." But the witch locked Beth in the cage. The witch got the treasure and ran away but Beth remembered she had the magic key so she opened the cage and ran away. When she was running she stepped on something sharp, it was a huge diamond. So she ran home and lived happily with her family. But as for the witch, she had the treasure box and no key.

How Was Your Day?
by Joe Daniels Parkin aged 11

"Come on, come on, how slow can you go? Grandma Johnson can run faster than you and she's dead!" The coach always picked on one kid, he was rubbish at sport, spelling and any task. Except art, he liked the colours and the wax crayons. He had a weird name, he was called Demetree Higawigon. "Demetree, count to three, have a good time in numeracy," the kids would chant. You see, numeracy was the worst task to Demetree. He was in the lowest group, lowest table, with the strictest teacher, Mrs Higawigon. Yes, you heard, Mrs Higawigon, she was Demetree's mother. He put up with her in school, and worse, at home. "Class... class... Shut up!" bellowed Mrs Higawigon, but to everyone else's surprise no-one was talking, she just wanted to see how high and loud her voice could go. "Is she still talking?" everyone asked, because nobody listened to her.

When numeracy had ended everyone went home. "Hi Dad," muttered Demetree, but nobody answered. Demetree took his bag off and went to the fridge. A note was on it:-

Dear Demetree

I've gone back to the lab, don't touch my transporter because it's armed.

He read it slowly, he didn't know and couldn't read transporter. And because of that, this is where the story begins.

Demetree went upstairs, gave his ball a kick, which bounced off the wall, hit Demetree's head, left him flying right into the transporter, which turned on, zapped Demetree and he had gone. Where he ended up, nobody knew, but the setting was a forest full of sand, twigs and snow. "Where am I?" wondered Demetree. Nobody answered but his echo repeated. He decided to look around, he made red Xs on the trees with his favourite wax crayon so he could see where he had been. He came to a village, a strange village, but it beckoned Demetree in a weird sort of way. A strange man came out of the long, narrow house. "Visitor," shouted the man. A thousand people came from the houses. "Hello," Demetree cried, sheepishly. "Your name young traveller?" "My name?" asked Demetree. "So art can be struct upon with art," said the man. Demetree didn't get a word he said but he heard the word art so he said, "Demetree." He went into the house where the man had come out of. "You draw," said the man and passed a pencil to Demetree and he drew a beautiful picture. Everyone was fascinated with his drawing, they knew what it was but looked more like it than Picasso's. A little boy looked at the drawing expectantly. He cried "Kit cat, colourful." He walked away and came back with a book full of cats. "Can Tranty have kitty cat picture in collection?" Demetree said, "Yeah, sure, whatever," and passed it to him and the boy walked away.

Demetree slowly went up to the old man and said, "How can I get home?" "Go to the great door by the sleeping snake of littleness, you must kill the snake of littleness."

"Easy, little snake."

"You use sword."

"OK, but I could use my finger… ha ha." So Demetree set off from the village to the snake of littleness. Demetree jogged over hill after hill, tripping up after tripping up, singing each song that could pop into his head. He came to the door where a gigantic snake stood, well not standing, what does a snake do? He was sleeping anyway. So Demetree sneaked past him and took the sword in the air to hit it, then it woke up. "Gulp."

Demetree swung the sword at him anyway and missed. But he ran into the door and disappeared into his room. "Demetree," shouted his mum. He ran downstairs. "Dinner's ready." They sat down and began to eat slowly. "Yum, yum, shepherds pie," said Demetree.

"So Demetree, what happened in your day because I went to a new school today?"

"You went to a new school?"

"Yes, really upsetting."

"Yeah! Really mum?"

"So how was your day?"

"Don't ask."

What Really Happened To Cinderella?
by Aoife O'Hara aged 8

I expect you know the story of Cinderella. What rubbish! A very nice fairy tale, but in real life? Impossible! I'm here to tell you about the true story. None of that Prince ride-away-with-his-princess sort of thing. What really happened.

Well, the first bit is sort of true, I suppose, but what happened to the father? Some say he died, but how could he die when his wife had just died? It would be quite a coincidence. But maybe he caught her disease. Perhaps he was a coward. So cowardly he didn't even have the courage to care for and save his own daughter! Or maybe he had a hard, cold heart and did not care for Cinderella one bit. But possibly the stepmother sent him packing, as if he were a bird eating her cherry. Cinderella, of course, would be the cherry. "I can look after Cinderella all myself," she would say. The stepmother didn't actually seem that bad. Apart from the fact that she made Cinderella work in the kitchen. In the kitchen! She did all of the other work. It's not fair how stepmothers and sisters, and I'm sure fathers, are mean in fairy tales.

Oh, I almost forgot, she wasn't called Cinderella. Well, not in real life anyway. Her name was Ella. She didn't sleep by the cinders at all. And there weren't even any cinders anyway. They had a gas fire. Although that sounds weird, it's true. I know this story was meant to be set ages ago when they didn't have gas fires, but they did, I've seen the house. It's a little cottage in America that costs ten dollars to go in, just like any castles or exhibitions. The first room is quite big. It has a big chair with a red velvet cushion that looks a little worn out and scruffy and a bronze body – which also looks old and dirty. Also, there was a fireplace with no fire in it. There was a grand piano and each of the keys had a black tinge all over it. Then, there was a wooden table with a small stool next to it. But what caught my attention was the painting above the table. It was a picture of what they called "A Handsome Prince", painted in pastel colours. He had a strange expression on his face, like he's thinking, but also mean and cheeky at the same time. His wig was very messy and had hairs sticking up. He had little curls hanging from his ears and a small crown on his head. The next room was the kitchen. Nothing much in there. But the first thing I noticed was the gas fire. I stood there for a moment before going upstairs. It was very posh. I don't know how else I can explain it. Anyway, back to the story. This bit is called THE BALL. A royal messenger came and gave them an invitation, it said:

Dear Villagers
You are invited to the castle as we are holding a Royal Ball. All the eligible maidens are to attend.
Yours sincerely
The King

So Ella went out and bought some glass, out of which she made two glass slippers. She wore them to the ball, but on the way the heels snapped – glass is not a very clever thing to make shoes out of. The ball was very nice. First the Prince came to the front holding a round ball. He stood there for half an hour. I suppose you could say that was very dull and boring. I would agree. At the end, all of the women crowded the Prince and tried to kiss him. All apart from Ella. She was the only girl with any common sense. But the Prince looked up and saw her. He smiled, showing all of his horrible black teeth. Ella ran, leaving one of her not so perfect glass slippers behind her. She was running because, to her, the Prince meant nothing but the man in the picture on her wall. The Prince cried and he looked worse than ever. There were tears running down his cheeks. His eyes were bright red. His mouth was wide open, showing all of his black teeth and sending spit dribbling down his chin. Also, his nose was very runny. Yuck! All of the women would lend him their hankie and try to cheer him up by saying false things like, "How could she run away from such a handsome man?" Then he started telling a false story about her knowing him all his life and she was just embarrassed. They would all shower him with kisses, the best they could. Then he saw the slipper. He was on it like a dart. "I will search until I find the owner of this shoe," he shouted.

When he finally found Ella's house, it didn't fit the mother (obviously). He tried it on Ella. It fitted perfectly. "Oh," she shouted, "I don't want to live with you! It sounds totally dull and boring, just like the ball was," and with that she waved to the stepmother and ran to the door, then she left.

Some say she ran off, regretting what she had just done. I can't tell you where she went, but I can tell you she never returned. And the Prince? Of course he cried. The stepmother told him that she wouldn't baby-sit a crying Prince, but she would marry one. He looked up at her and blew his nose, "OK," he replied. And so, plans were made and she is still living with him today.

I Want To Explore Space
by Robyn Farrell aged 8

Sophie was bored, she'd played with all her toys and all her friends were on holiday. She wished she was on holiday too. Sophie started dreaming bout where she would like to go. She quite fancied Spain or France or maybe the moon even. When she was little she always wanted to be an astronaut. She decided to go to the park to get some fresh air. A new climbing frame had been put up. It looked a bit like a flying saucer. Sophie looked inside and saw a boy who looked like an alien. He smiled and said, "Hello." Sophie ran hot-foot out of the park. The alien ran after her, he managed to catch up. "I will take you on a journey through space."

Sophie always dreamt of flying through space but then he could be tricking her, you never can tell with aliens. Anyway, she gave him a chance. Sophie followed him back to the saucer. When she had just stepped in, the flying saucer took off! Sophie tried very hard not to fall. "First stop, the moon," said the alien. Well, Sophie never thought it would be so quick to go to the moon. The alien (who was called Dido) said to be careful, that in the month of July the moon is often known to crack from top to bottom. Sophie had to have breathing powder put on as it is harder to breathe in space. Sophie found it was rather hard to walk in space. She and Dido explored the planet, not in detail as it would take years, but they saw most of the best bits, like the man in the moon. Suddenly, the whole planet shook and, where Sophie and Dido stood, a crack started breaking, getting bigger every second and Sophie started falling, followed by Dido, and they fell from top to bottom and landed….. on Mars.

Sophie had no idea where they were at first but Dido knew it was Mars. "Dido," Sophie asked, "what are those strange things over there?" Dido stopped and stood as still as a stone statue. "Those? They are Flamingphantraffes. Run!" Dido cried. Him and Sophie ran like cheetahs. Sophie was amazed at the animals' names. A Flamingphantraffe! It was nothing compared to what they looked like though. Its head was like a flamingo, its body was like an elephant and its legs were like a giraffe's. Sophie and Dido ran like mad. Dido shouted, "Jump," at her as he did it himself. As he jumped he floated into the air. "It's the gravity pulling me up," Dido said, as Sophie was looking confused. Sophie realised then and did it herself. She followed Dido back to the space ship. Sophie and Dido decided to go back to the park as Sophie would be a bit late. About eighteen years later Sophie got a job as an astronaut. She passed her tests easily as Dido had shown her everything about a space ship and the Moon and Mars.

The Old Cricket Field
by Daniel Lomas aged 10

"Who is he?" said Joe, "That boy's been watching us practice all year!"

"I don't know who he is but, yes, he is getting a bit annoying," said Mark.

"Every time we go into the pavilion to speak to him he has disappeared," moaned Alex (he was the one who came up with the plans they used in their matches, but wasn't the captain, Joe was).

The boys were too caught up in the mystery of the stranger to keep track of time. Before they realised it, Christmas had passed by and they needed to start practising for the school cricket tournament. They pushed the memory of the boy to the back of their minds and concentrated harder.

"Do you reckon we're gonna win this year?" asked Joe, during a practice session. Suddenly, they felt the familiar foreboding feeling and they glanced up at the usual pallid face at the window. "Of course we wi…," began Mark, but they all froze as an ear-splitting scream cut through the air. Everyone gasped. Alex was on the ground moaning in pain and, kneeling next to him was …

"Archie," said the boy, "my name is Archie. I know we don't know each other but this boy is in terrible pain."

Even though he looked normal, the boy seemed to have a sadness around him, his voice was a mere whisper, but they still caught every word.

"Why haven't you spoken to us before?" asked Joe, finally finding his voice, "Or even come out to see us?"

"It was too light. I stay inside since…." Suddenly, everyone realised that, while they were talking, night had begun to fall.

"So, we should get Alex home now," Mark said, moving over to him and lifting him to his feet. "Where does it hurt?"

"I think I've b..b..broken my ank..k..kle," stuttered Alex, who seemed very close to tears, but was holding them back determinedly. They helped him limp home, but now they were one player short. "Mmm … Archie?" shouted Joe suddenly, giving everyone a start, even Archie who was walking quite a bit ahead.

"Yes?"

"Since Alex can't play, can you play in his place?"

"Er, hmmm, okay," he agreed finally.

"Okay, be at the cricket field tomorrow."

"Don't worry, I will."

Sure enough, when they arrived there he was, waiting to get started.

"I thought you said you hate the light," remembered Mark.

"Oh, that's just, just because I'm, I'm.... ill."

"Why?"

"I can't tell you that, now let's get practising."

They practised until the sun set and they found out that Archie was very good indeed, extremely good in fact. The match with the other school was the next day. It was very important as it was the final. The boys decided on an early night, said goodbye to each other and watched as Archie walked away on his own.

"Hey, Archie, got far to go? My dad can give you a lift," Joe shouted after him. Archie turned.

"No, it's okay, I'll see you tomorrow." He turned back and then he'd gone. Monday arrived. The school cricket was later that afternoon. All of the boys were excited but nervous at the same time.

"I hope Archie turns up. It was a good thing we were allowed one player not from our school, he's a real star!" Joe said, "Perhaps he'll join the team permanently."

The team won with flying colours, thanks to Archie who was a great player. The presentation of the cup was made and Joe and the rest of the team turned to thank Archie, but he'd already gone!

"Where's Archie, where is he?"

They looked everywhere and even when everyone had gone, they still couldn't find him, he wasn't even in the pavilion! They saw an old man who was helping to tidy the ground.

"We can't find Archie anywhere," Mark said to him anxiously, "Do you know him? We wanted to thank him, invite him to play all the time."

The man looked surprised, "Archie, Archie who plays cricket?"

"Yes, do you know him?"

"I did know an Archie, years ago, fifty years ago it must be, I used to play in the same team. Brilliant he was, would have played for England eventually. Sadly he died, terrible, terrible. He got hit on the head with a cricket ball, never regained consciousness."

The boys looked stunned. The old man continued, "Some people say he's here, everywhere, especially in the pavilion, haunting it, but if it's true I know he's just watching the cricket."

"But he played! Archie played in our team! We won! We won!"

The boys still played cricket, won some and lost some. They always looked up at the pavilion windows and waved. You know, if you looked closely on a sunny summer evening, you might have just seen Archie watching the game he loved so much.

The House Of Ghosts
by Abby Leck aged 11

Emily's heart was thumping so fast she felt it would come tearing through her rib-cage at any moment, she had never done so much running in her life. Pete felt ill and he had a killer stitch in one side. They wished they'd never gone anywhere near that stupid mansion, with its grimy windows and rusty door. Why couldn't they have just stayed away, gone in the other direction they thought, then they wouldn't have to keep on running when their feet ached so much. But curiosity had got the better of them. It had all just been one big nightmare, but it was real, they were sure of it, the pains from the running were all too, well, painful for a dream. This is the story of what happened, the story that neither of them would forget for as long as they lived.

It had been just a normal, sunny summer's day in the small mountain town of Dervensky. Birds were singing in the trees and the sun was brightly shining in the clear blue sky, where the few clouds up there were fluffy and frosty like icing-sugar, and everyone wore a smile. Emily and Pete decided it was a perfect day to climb one of the tall, rocky mountains surrounding Dervensky. There were only a few which they had not yet explored, one of these being Great Clumbasin, the biggest mountain out of all of them, in fact, so big you couldn't even see the top. They packed a picnic and set off. It was a tough climb and involved a lot of scrambling and scrabbling around for any cracks they could wedge their hands and feet in. After climbing at least halfway up the mountain, they stopped for a rest.

"I'm puffed!" exclaimed Pete.

"Yes, that climb was MUCH harder than I expected, it's so steep!" admitted Emily.

"Can I have a ham butty yet?" Pete begged, "I'm STARVING."

"Hey, I want a jam one but we've got to save them 'til we get to the top, well if we DO get to the top," Emily replied, always the sensible one.

And, with that, Peter ruffled his soft hazel coloured hair, making it stick up like a duckling's downy feathers. Emily flicked back her long luxurious blonde hair, to stop it tickling the back of her neck, and they carried on up, towards their destination – the top of the mountain.

"Why – don't – we – go – back – now?" Pete suggested.

"Don't you want the satisfaction of saying you've climbed Great Clumbasin?" Emily stated, knowing Peter couldn't say no to that.

Sure enough, after some consideration, Pete nodded and they carried on. Despite the scraping of shins on the jagged rocks, it was a beautiful climb and the thought of the view at the top kept them going. But as they neared the top, a cold wind grew, whipping their faces and burning their cheeks. They could barely see as their hair was blown across their faces. All the cheerful noises of Dervensky disappeared behind them, as if sucked in by a giant hurricane. Instead, the howling winds whirled around in their ears. As the children looked down, they realised there was just a thick fog, they had no choice but to go upwards.

That was when they saw it. The mansion. There it was, looming above them, when suddenly the howling winds were gone – just like that, as if someone had pulled out a giant plug, sucking them down. The children gazed at the mansion, it looked scary and deserted but, being young, carefree and careless, Emily and Pete were itching to explore. Peter stepped forward and pushed open the door. It opened with an eerie squeak, revealing a large empty hallway. Pete edged in and beckoned to Emily to do the same. She took a deep breath and, biting her nails in a nervous state, she took small steps towards the door. She was deeply regretting ever agreeing to enter the mansion.

Once inside, their footsteps were hollow and echoed around the room as they made their way across to see what they could uncover. Suddenly some arms protruded out of the wall and grabbed Emily, pulling her through. Pete rushed forward to help her, but when he touched the wall it was rock hard!

"Emily, Emily, where are you?" he called out desperately.

He knew he must go after her, but which way to go? He opened the door nearest to him but it was just a small room containing nothing but a chair. He tried the next door, it was a broom cupboard, but as he was about to close it again he thought he saw a taught, pale face looming out of the darkness.

"Stay awaaaaay!!!" she warned, her voice eerie, "I was foolish enough to enter this mansion and look what happened to meeee!" She swooped out so Pete could get a full view of her. He surveyed her body, up and down, she was as pale as the full moon on a cloudless night.

"What happened?" he asked.

"It was Jake!" she explained, "He is the ghost of the man who once lived here, he is protective of his old property and he turned me into – THIS! Just because I wanted to take a look at this here mansion. If I were you, I'd find your friend and get out!"

"But who are you?"

"My name is Maureen. I was just 37 when I died, but now I'm 2536."

Pete did not know which way to go though, but as he stood puzzling as to where he should go, he heard a long moaning sound. It was coming from down a long corridor and, as the sound came bouncing off the walls, it echoed, sounding like the cries of a million children. He followed the sound and it led him into a large room, full of objects covered in big, white sheets. He noticed a tremble under one of them and whipped the sheet off. Emily was tied up underneath it with a piece of tape stuck over her mouth. Pete helped her to her feet and pulled the tape from her mouth.

"Come on then," he insisted, forgetting what Maureen had told him, "Let's explore this house some more."

"I – I don't know," she replied, "I'd rather just get out of here now and not stay."

"You wuss!" he jeered, "Oh hang on, I forgot, you're a girl, girls are natural wusses."

"You shut up, girls are just as brave as boys! Braver actually!" she shouted and she marched off moodily towards the nearest door.

But before she could reach it, it was suddenly flung open. Emily screamed and, as she tried to run away, she found to her terror that she was paralysed to the spot. An evil cackle came from somewhere in the room, making Emily and Pete jump with fright, their eyes darting around trying to identify the source of the noise. "Why hello, I don't think we've met. Let me introduce myself – I'm Jake," boomed the wicked voice of a scrawny male ghost, swooping out of the room behind the door. That was when all that Maureen had warned him of came flooding back to Pete, but before he could do anything Jake had gathered him and Emily up and swept them off into the room he'd originally come from. He shoved them both down on some chairs and snakes came out of what seemed like nowhere and began binding themselves around the children's wrists, ankles and all over their bodies.

The children were unable to move and the snakes looked poisonous.

Jake whipped out a carving knife and cackled evilly, "This, children, is the end. Ha ha ha ha!"

When, from a room somewhere upstairs, there came a loud clanging noise and some creepy, high pitched singing. No matter how hard they strained their ears they couldn't quite make out the words being sung, but Jake could. He jerked and writhed and swooshed out of the room with an almighty shriek.

"Quick children, you must run as far as you can away from this place," Maureen told them as she swooped through the wall and hurriedly began to tame the snakes, she then clicked her fingers and the snakes shrivelled down in size until they became little worms. "Now hurry."

The children did not need to be told again and, as soon as they were free, they flung open all the doors they went through, burst outside and legged it as fast as they could.

And so we come back to the beginning of our story, as for Emily and Pete, they scrambled down the mountainside, tumbling at times, but not stopping otherwise. And when they came to the thick mist they didn't stop, they were sucked down into the fog. It is unknown what really happened to them in there as they never emerged. They never got to report their triumph over climbing the Great Clumbasin. But remember, there is a lesson to be learnt, if you ever decide to climb a mountain one fine summer's day and there is a mansion up at the top – DO NOT ENTER!

My Life Saver
by Olivia Ashley aged 10

I opened my eyes and looked around. I was on a beach. I suddenly remember what happened. I was on a cliff, on a wall. I remember me screaming and that's it. What happened next, what happened before? My mind is blank, I can't remember anything except that scream. I stood up slowly and blinked my eyes, I saw a blurred figure so I blinked again. It was a man, he said that his name was William, he helped me. He asked me what happened, but I couldn't remember anything. He asked me who my parents were, but I couldn't remember. He took me to the doctors, they explained what happened. I told the doctor that my head was hurting, he did an x-ray and told me that I wouldn't be able to remember anything and would have to learn how to do things over again.

William was trying to find out who my parents were. He said that he would look after me until we find them. Every day I would go to a special school which would help me remember things. I liked going there and I made progress.

One day, I sat there in my chair and I thought really hard and I saw her, my mum. I ran down to see

William with a beaming smile on my face. He smiled back. I ran up to him and I got a piece of paper and a pen and began to draw. I was a very good drawer now. William asked me what I was drawing. I didn't answer until I had finished. I gave it to him and said "It's my mum." "What?" said William, surprised. "I remember my mum," I said, getting so excited. "That's great," he said, with a beaming smile on his face too.

I knew what to do, I drew lots of copies of the picture. I had to ask William to write our phone number because I couldn't write then. I was making posters, I was going to stick them around town. The very next day I started to stick them on shop windows, on street lights, on phone boxes. I stuck them everywhere. William helped me.

The whole of the next day I sat by the phone, I didn't go to my special school. Then the next day I did the same, and then the day after that I still sat there waiting. I never got a phone call, so the next day William sent me to school. He said that he would tell me if he got the call. He didn't. It was at least a week until someone called. I picked it up, I was excited, too excited. I gave the phone to William and sat there listening to their conversation. William put the phone down and smiled. I knew the answer and gave him a big smile and hugged him. I thought this was the happiest day of my life. I ran to my room and sat on my bed and I realised, what will happen to William? Would I ever see him again? I sat there for a bit, then I heard a knock on the door. It was William, he sat next to me and said, "Your mum will pick you up at two o'clock." He walked and opened the door then turned around and said, "I'll miss you," then went.

At five to two I went downstairs and waited by the door. It was ten past when I heard a knock. I was trembling, shaking all over, knees knocking. I was nervous, but I opened the door and tried to smile. Mum wasn't the same, her hair had grown, but I knew it was her because of the way she looked at me. I said bye to William, he smiled, but you could tell he was about to cry.

Mum took me home. I looked at my room, it was just the way I had left it. The next day I went to school. Mum picked me up. I asked to go to William's house, she let me. I rang the bell, he answered and I stood there and smiled. I went to his house on Saturday after school. I did this every weekend. My memory came back after a while and William taught me new things, like how to write. He helped me to draw as well. He's an excellent drawer, he said I will be an artist when I grow up. I am actually quite glad I fell off the cliff. I got the best of both worlds, I've got my mum who loves me more now and William, who is one of my best friends. My life saver.

The Amazing Gnome
by Lucy Ryan aged 11

Long ago in a town called Smivle Hill there lived a gnome, but not just any old gnome, this gnome had a beard as long as his living room. It was so big that his friends came just to see his beard. He thought they came to see him, but the trouble was they always say, "I love your beard."

One day he got so sick of the same question that he decided to wait for the next person to come and ask him whether he comes to see him or the beard. He sat in his chair glaring around the room, wondering what is going to happen next? For hours nobody came and then there was a knock at the door and in came a rich but small king. Firstly, they had a chat and then they went for a walk beside a fast flowing river. Also, the queen was there. Suddenly the king slipped and fell into the river. Nobody had a rope, it was awful to see. Cautiously he thought, then he flung his beard into the water. The king grabbed onto it and was heaved to the side.

After, they went back to the gnome's house to have a cup of dandelion tea. The gnome was given a reward for helping the king. To this day, we never know the gnome's name, for it still remains a secret as the gnome didn't want to be famous.

The Three Eyed Rat's Evil Plan
by Kendal Thompson aged 10

In a dark, dark forest there lived a three eyed rat. All the rat did all day was eat and sleep, he was a very lazy rat. But he always caused problems and arguments, which he found very amusing! The place he got food from was awful. On a weekday he would get it from someone's house and on a weekend he would scuttle into a dirty, rotten old skip in search of food.

He lived in a wheelie bin, where he could also find food. The wheelie bin was in someone's back garden with all his ratty three eyes family. His job was to wreck people's lives.

One day, his family were all still sleeping so he decided to go out on a wild adventure and, while he was there, he thought he might just wreck a few lives. So he set off on his adventure through the forest. He saw one little cottage which looked like one in a story book and he said, "I think I shall have a shot wrecking the people's lives who live here." The rat found a crack in the door and decided to make his way through there. As soon as he got in, he started to check if anyone was in and it seemed to be that no-one was, so he thought what he could do. Then he thought he could go and get the rest of his family and they could all hide and wait until the family came back and they could scare the family and, if we keep coming back, they might even have the urge to move homes! We could even hide in their beds!

He decided he would go back to his wheelie bin now and start planning where he could hide, so he scuttled off through the front door.

His family agreed to do the evil plan, so the next day they all set off on the journey over to the cottage. They had decided that they would take some props which they could use for more fright factor, like gunge and mould that had come off their bodies, and they could splatter it all around the cottage. Later that day, the plan had all been set up and arranged and now all they had to do was wait for their rivals. They were waiting for around an hour, but then the owners were just unlocking the cottage and everyone got into their places, but one thing the rats didn't know was that the owners loved strange creatures and they had been waiting all their lives to see a weird creature, so the rats were up for a surprise! The owners entered the house and the woman screamed to death and the man was about to faint until... he saw the rats and he was thrilled with joy and so was his wife. The owners ran up to the rats and they were crying with joy. The rats just ran out of the house and they never tried to ruin anyone's life ever again, in case they got humiliated again. The rat family never stepped foot out of the wheelie bin ever again.

Cluedo

by Joseph Woods aged 9

It all started two days ago in the little town of Glossop. I was sitting there reading the morning newspaper when, suddenly, I heard a gun-shot and about a second after the shot, a scream. I got up and ran as fast as I could to the crime scene. Someone had been shot!!! And it looked like murder! I thought to myself, I'm going to find out who had done it. My first idea was to find out who had been killed. It was Mr Van the greengrocer. Next, to find out why. My first thought was maybe he saw something he was not meant to see. My first suspect was Dan, he had just got out of prison and, if he had done it, he would be going back for a very long time. After I had asked him some questions he proved not guilty. My next suspect was Hazel Woods, she was a housewife and, after I asked a few questions, proved not guilty. Then suddenly the door burst open and someone stepped inside, they had nearly collapsed, but they sat down and said, "I know who the murderer is." I said, "Who?" They said, "The vicar." I said, "What, the vicar did it, how do you know?" "Well, no-one goes to church any more and the vicar has nearly lost his job so, to get all the people back to church, he would have a funeral and he wouldn't lose his job."

So, we interviewed the vicar and he proved guilty and that is how we caught the murderer from Glossop.

A Mothers Day Present
by Abigail Crossman aged 10

"I'm going to work, now you two be good because you will be spending the whole morning on your own, take Spot for a walk too and, oh yes, do not open the door to strangers. I'll be back home at dinner time, bye-bye."

"Bye-bye Mum," shouted both children, Tom and Kayleigh.

It was the day before Mothers Day and Tom and Kayleigh needed to buy their mum a present, so they got their shoes and coats on and attached Spot's lead to his red, stripy collar and set off walking to the chocolate shop. "Come on Kayleigh, we need to get there fast, we only have an hour and a half to get Mum some roses and her favourite chocolates."

"Tom, we're here, come on Spot. Hello, have you got any of those caramel chocolates in the star shaped boxes?" said Kayleigh anxiously. "Yes, we did, we sold out an hour ago."

"Oh dear, what are we going to do Tom?"

"We'll have some of those pink roses please," asked Tom very politely. "Come on Kayleigh, we are going to search everywhere, every shop."

The children searched everywhere, but they didn't find the chocolates. They have five minutes to get home because then Mum will be back from work. "Let's get the bus to Jelly Road and there's a chocolate shop there, it's worth a try but it means that we'll be late home and we might get told off by Mum." Just then Kayleigh's mobile rang. "Hello."

"Hello Kayleigh, tell Tom I will be a little bit late home, perhaps ten minutes, the traffic is bad."

"OK Mum, bye. Tom, we have got an extra ten minutes, Mum's stuck in traffic," said Kayleigh excitedly.

"Right, we better get a move on."

The children go into the shop and....

"Found it," cried Tom.

The children ran home with Spot just in time to wrap their presents and hide them. In the morning the children gave their mum her presents and told her all about their day.

At The Water's Edge
by Milly Price aged 11

As I stand here in the soft sand, grains between my toes, I think about how I lost everything. In the distance the old, battered fence is worn and won't last much longer. I used to think I couldn't go on. Not anymore. After my experience I could tackle any challenge...

It was a merry life on board our ship, "The Emily May". Each night drinks would be served and not a soul wasn't up and dancing. The taste of chilled alcohol stayed in our throats, although it wasn't quite the same the next day with our heavy heads and droopy eyes. Apart from that, nothing got us down.

One particular night was awful, awful yet memorable. It was my turn to throw over the anchor and I felt weak, like a helpless, starving dog. As I threw the anchor into the murky, mysterious ocean, I went with it. I tried shouting for help but no-one could hear me. The sea's hands grabbed me and took me under with all its might. As I came back up I could smell the salt water in the back of my throat. I tried reaching out for something but the only thing I could touch was the rough ripples surrounding me. The only thing I could do, apart from pray, was to struggle; struggle for dear life.

I soon found myself washed up on a deserted beach and knew that there I would spend the rest of my days. As I stand here at the water's edge not knowing what is ahead of me, all I can do is imagine.

Break Up
by Laura Gilbert aged 9

A few years ago, in 2002, there was a young girl named Louise. She was 10 years old and had a little brother named Liam who was 8 years old. Their parents, Vicky and John, were kind and loving. All until – SMASH! John had dropped and smashed Vicky's £3,000 diamond necklace. That's when the real trouble began.

"Aarghhh!" screamed Vicky, "My necklace."

"Aarghhh!" screamed John, "My hand!" (as he had cut his hand on a tiny shard of glistening diamond).

"Mum," shouted Louise, "what's wrong?"

"Dad," shouted Liam, "what's wrong?"

"Your father," growled Vicky, "just smashed my £3,000 diamond necklace into tiny little bits. That's what's wrong."

"Go upstairs kids, we need to have a private talk," explained John.

Ten minutes passed by. "Kids, come down now," shouted Vicky. They came down.

"Your mother and I," John said in a very serious tone of voice, "your mother and I have decided to get a divorce."

"Nooo, you can't, you just can't, I won't accept it, it's not allowed, think how much you love each other! This can't be happening to me," cried Liam. Louise was just sitting there, staring blankly at her parents. "I'm afraid it can," she said quietly. Small beads of tears ran down her cold, pale face. "I'm so sorry," said Vicky, "but it is for the best."

"I'm moving out tomorrow," explained John.

Louise couldn't take it anymore, she ran upstairs crying her eyes out.

Three days later, John had moved out and Louise and Liam were up in their den. They were thinking of a solution to get their parents back together. "I have an idea," Louise piped up, "but it will be risky. We'll have to borrow Mum's video camera. I will sneak out to Dad's house with the video camera and film Dad for three days. He's bound to be miserable on his own. You do the same with your video camera to Mum. She's been looking lonely. I'll then creep back to the house with the tape and we'll show it to Mum. You do the same, but sneak out to Dad's house.

"Wow," exclaimed Liam, "that's brilliant. But how will we sneak out without Mum noticing?"

"Oh yeah," Louise exclaimed, "I didn't think of that." They sat for about 4 more seconds until Louise spoke again. "Mum hardly ever sees us anymore because she's so miserable. We wake up and Mum's still asleep, have breakfast, go out to school, school ends and we come home, but Mum's out doing something and she doesn't come home until way after we go to bed, she just leaves stuff on the table for tea."

"Yeah," said Liam. "OK, let's do it tonight."

Later that night, Louise had already snuck out and Liam was busy setting up the camera in the living room, while Louise had just snuck into the back of her Dad's house.

A week later, Louise caught the bus back to the house and they swapped over houses.

This is what is going on in John's house. "Er, Dad?"

"Yes son?"

"Erm, I have a video for you to watch. Tell me what you think of it." Minutes pass by then, "Oh my goodness, is this how much your mother's been grieving. I've got to get over there, come on Liam."

Back at the house. "Erm, Mum?"

"Yes Louise?"

"Erm, I have a video for you to watch. Tell me what you think of it."

Minutes pass by then, "Oh my goodness, is this how much your father's been grieving? I feel so sorry for him."

Ding dong! "I'll get it," said Louise.

"I LOVE YOU," shouted John.

"I LOVE YOU TOO," shouted Vicky.

Daniel And The Game Of Chess
by Anna Katherine Hart aged 8

"Hi Ted," said Daniel as soon as he was awake. Ted was Daniel's teddy. He liked to talk to his teddy, also he liked to play on his computer. His favourite computer game was called "Aliens Coming To Invade". One thing that he really didn't like was playing board games.

As soon as he had got ready and had his breakfast, he turned on his computer and played his games but, after a bit, he got bored and decided to have a look at some different web-sites. He clicked some buttons and a box came up on the screen saying, "Play your game of chess against the computer, a great board game for all of the family".

Daniel didn't even read the box and just pressed, "Yes". When the board appeared on the screen and the pieces were sorting themselves out into their places, Daniel just kept clicking and clicking. Suddenly, to his surprise, a hand reached out of the computer and sucked him into it.

Daniel found himself in a place that had a big, giant board of chess. Daniel was standing beside it. It was unbelievable. Now you know that Daniel had never played chess before because it was a board game and Daniel hated board games. He didn't want to play chess, even though he knew he might like it a lot.

Daniel was now staring at the stranger standing on the other side of the chess board. The man said, "My name is Kevin, though many people call me Kev." There was a sudden silence. Then Daniel managed to spit out, "My name is Daniel. Shall I run across to you?" Kevin replied, "Yes." So Daniel ran across the chess board as fast as he could.

When he finally got to the other side he was out of breath. The man said he was going to teach him to play chess. Although Daniel hated chess, he thought the man was kind to teach him how to play chess, so he carried on listening to what Kevin had to say. He named all the pieces, the Pawn, the Castle, the Knight, the Bishop, the Queen and the King. He also explained how they moved. He said that the Pawns only move forwards and can only take diagonally, they can move two on their first go or one if they choose and all of their other goes they can only move one space. The Castle moves any number of squares but only moves to the side or front of them. The Knight moves two squares in front and one to the side or one in front of it and two to the side. The Bishop moves any number of spaces diagonal. The Queen can move like the Castle and the Bishop. The King moves in any direction but only one square at a time.

Daniel had listened very carefully to the instructions and thought that it sounded good after all. Kevin said a few things about check and check-mate, then he asked if Daniel would like to play chess against him. Daniel sounded very eager whilst saying, "Yes please." So they both stood beside their pieces and started to move. Each time they did a move they had to lift up the heavy pieces and carry them to where they wanted it. You could hear the voices saying, "Check," "Check," "Check." Then Daniel suddenly moved his Queen and said "CHECK MATE!" He couldn't believe he'd won. Kevin thanked Daniel for playing and congratulated him for winning. Daniel asked if he could go back to his house, so Kevin took him back to his house.
POOF!
He appeared sitting in front of his computer. Kevin had left him a chess board and pieces so he could play at home. Daniel took the board downstairs and made his mum play and he won! His mum asked him, "Where did you get this board from? How did you learn to play? Where have you been all this time? I thought you didn't like board games!" We know... don't we!!

The School Bag
by Katy Waddell aged 11

I was running, running as fast as I could. I tripped, I was falling. I felt pain all over my body. I heard the crash of glass, I screamed. I looked at my legs, there was blood everywhere, lots of blood. Next I heard the sound of sirens. I felt frightened and afraid. Then I heard the words, "It's alright Jen, we're here." I was carried into this van like I was being kidnapped and I couldn't get out. I heard the siren noise again. I bet you are wondering how this all started...

Well, it started when I was walking home from school. I could hear heavy footsteps behind me. I turned round, I couldn't see that clearly because it was dark. I could see a tall, thin figure. I could tell he was wearing gel because I could see the outline of his hair. He was running. I could see something in his hand. It looked like a….. OH NO!!! I started running. I turned round, he was running too. I ran as fast as I could. I turned round, I heard him say, "Oi." I was approaching a block of flats. I ran up the stairs, they were really steep, there must have been at least 200 of them. I neared the last few. I was getting tired. My heart was beating faster than it ever had before. I came to the top of the flats, up to the roof. I suddenly tripped, I started falling, it hurt, it was painful, I thought that was going to be it.

Now I'm in here lying in a bed. There are lots of people here. I feel like I'm a hostage. Hang on a minute, I recognise that silhouette. He is approaching me, that man from last night. "Help! Help!" I scream. Oh no, he's got a school bag in his hand.

"Hello," he said.

"H..H..Hello," I stammered.

"You forgot your school bag. I tried to give it to you yesterday but you ran away from me, sorry if I scared you."

All this pain and trouble over a forgotten school bag.

Sweet Dreams
by Lucy Potts aged 11

Do you ever feel unsafe? Or as if someone is watching your every move? Have you ever heard someone, but when you turned around no-one was there? If you have, it's best not to visit the Shambular Hotel!

Katie and Lucy looked at the shattered hotel standing ashamed in front of them. "Do you think it's..."

"Haunted? No, of course not," replied Katie, looking down at the ground.

They entered the scary excuse for a hotel, after all they were soaking and all they wanted was a little rest. Katie looked down at her trendy and drenched Nike shoes. "Oh bother, I'm soaked," yelled Katie, giving a glum look down at her jeans.

"Hello, welcome to Shambular Hotel, how long do you wish to share your presence?" quizzed Laura the manager. She was a long, thin figure with long, blonde hair.

"You what?" replied Lucy. Katy elbowed her in the ribs.

"Terribly sorry about my rude friend. We'll just be staying one night please."

"Ok. You're in Room 24, enjoy your stay," said Sarah, the manager's assistant, in a creepy manner. She again had long, blonde hair and was a tall, thin figure.

"There was something strange about those women," Lucy said, bashing her bag against the wall.

"To be honest, I really don't care, I just want a rest," exclaimed Katie, yawning broadly.

Early the next morning, they woke up, it was pitch black. The girls crept downstairs, no-one was to be seen or heard, apart from a dirty, black rat and a peculiar, old woman. "It wasn't like this yesterday, unless they got a 60 minute makeover," called Lucy as her voice echoed around the dark hall.

"It's almost as if we've gone back in time. Let's ask this lady," said Katie.

"Excuse me, but could you tell me what the year is and where the hotel manager and assistant are?" asked Lucy.

"Hah, are you kidding, it's year 1947 and the manager and assistant died 10 years ago."

Lucy and Katie looked at each other, they looked back and the woman was gone. On the rear wall there was some strange writing, it was written in, no it couldn't be, blood? The writing read, "llik ot gniog ma I yadot".

Exactly! It was gobbledygook.

"I want to get out of this place, it's really creepy," muttered Katie.

"How did we get back in time anyway?" asked Lucy.

"Knowing your clumsiness, you probably did something wrong," replied Katie.

Lucy lent against the rusty brown wall and, all of a sudden, they were leaning against the paying desk. They must have gone back to normal again. They turned around and saw the same old lady again.

"Excuse me, but do you know where the manager and the assistant are?" Lucy quizzed.

"Yes, and I also know that they will never be coming back," said the old lady with an evil glint in her eye.

Cremating The Living
by Fay Marsden aged 10

I used to look forward to my birthday, it used to be the highlight of my year, it used to, but now I fear it! I remember it as if I was living through it again, every 8th October...

It was the 7th October and I was jumping up and down with excitement – literally! I ran downstairs to Nan and, before I could even get to her, I had a card thrust into my hand.

I never saw who gave it to me and, at that moment, I didn't care. I tore open the card and scrutinised every detail to deduce who it was from, for the sender's name was not there. The card read as follows:-

Dear Zinna (my name)

Happy Death-Day

For a moment I did not realise what was wrong, then I realised when I couldn't link the handwriting to a family friend or member. Then Nan came over and babbled on about "one more day" in her Nanna way, so I hid the card and said it was junk mail.

At school Mr Hilton told us about an "Around Town" bus trip with school, for tomorrow. We didn't know the date when he first told us. Then it struck me, like a 1 tonne weight to the head. The death-day card, could it mean I was to die on the trip? A shiver ran up my spine, I was sure that was what it meant.

The day finally came for the trip, I tried and failed in many desperate attempts to stay home, but no such luck. I was tense and wary. I followed superstition rule, but I still felt that I was about to die. On arrival, I said goodbye to all my friends from other classes and slowly took what seemed to be the last glimpse of my school and my childhood friends.

The details of what happened next I have forgotten, my guess is that it was so horrific I've blotted it from my memory. But I do know there was a crash!

Everyone thought I was dead. They were wrong, I was simply knocked out. When my Nan arrived she was in floods of tears. She rushed me back home and laid me in a large drawer with a blanket beneath me. She lit 11 candles around (for 11 was my new age) and dropped them on us both. "We'll burn together," she cried.

I woke up screaming in the drawer, everything around, including me, was in full flame. Nan was gone in a few seconds, my whole world went black.

When help finally came, I was nothing but ash and rubble. Now every 8th October there is a terrible screaming and smell of burning flesh in that same spot. So, if you get a card thrust into your hands the day before your birthday... DROP IT!... don't unlock the death-day curse.

The Forbidden Chamber
by Rebecca Helliwell aged 10

Who should ever dare to read this tale must be warned, this story could give you nightmares for the rest of your miserable life. It all started in a dilapidated house with mildew in every nook and cranny. Unfortunately for the residents of this so-called dwelling, the garden is a graveyard. These poor, helpless residents are Aunt Gertrude, a sly and selfish excuse for a human, and Annie, who shall now tell you a tale about a peculiar happening that changed her life forever.

One abnormal day, while I was sat reading a book about "Ghosts & Ghouls", I began to recall my Aunt saying never to enter the little room which can be entered by a mouse-size door in the far corner of my room.

Without thinking about all the possibilities, I opened the tiny door and peered inside to find complete and utter darkness. So I grabbed a burning candle as quick as a flash and slid inside. When I stood up I heard a little voice in my head (I think it was common sense) saying, "Turn back quick or it'll be too late." I realised how stupid I had been, I was as curious as a toddler with a new toy. I darted towards the exit to find it was bolted. My head began to sweat, I felt a wet tear trickle down my cold cheek, it was as if I had turned as blind as a bat, and all I could see was the faint glimmer of the candle, struggling to stay alight in the faint breeze coming from the cracked window.

Suddenly, I felt the feeling as if someone was watching me (you know the feeling when you wake up in the middle of the night, when you need a drink you get out of bed and walk across the landing very quietly, trying not to wake your Dad, then you hear a door creaking so you grab a book out of the bookcase and hold it ready to hit anything that moves, then you see a shadow but you find its just your Dad going to the toilet). But that was not the case because I couldn't see anything. My hair stood on end, I could feel someone's warm breath on my neck. I was as scared as a mouse ready to be devoured by a famished cat. There was a loud thumping noise, it was my heart, I thought it was going to explode.

"Who... who... whose... there?" I murmured. I could

hear a faint shuffling sound.

Then a ghostly white hand shot out of the pitch black clouds and grabbed my shoulder and pulled me back into the black, never-ending darkness.

Annie got dragged into a small cellar where she was devoured by rats and spiders. You can wonder whose hand grabbed her for no-one ever knew.

As for Aunt Gertrude, she just went about her daily business and never noticed that poor Annie had died, so that just shows how stingy she really was.

So you just remember never to enter a forbidden chamber or you may never return.

Little Blue Riding Hood
by Jessica Roxburgh aged 10

One day in a big doughnut in Google Forest, a little girl called Blue Riding Hood was cooking cakes for her best friend's (Wolf) party. "Are you ready yet," screamed Motherhood (who looked a little like the ugly stepsister in Cinderella). "Yes, I'm ready," replied Blue Riding Hood, just about to skip through the door.

"Don't forget, don't talk to the Big Bad Grandmother," shouted Motherhood, waving goodbye at the door. "I won't," answered Blue Riding Hood. So Blue Riding Hood went skipping to her friend's house, when suddenly the big bad Grandmother jumped out from a bush (actually the bush was candy floss).

"Where are you going my pet?" questioned

Grandmother, with her fake teeth ready to gobble up Blue Riding Hood.

"I'm going to Wolf's party in that big bun cake over there," answered Blue Riding Hood, while pointing to a big bun cake in the distance.

"Thank you pet, now run along," thanked Grandmother, pushing Blue Riding Hood towards the bun cake. What a nice lady, but there was something familiar. "Oh well," said Blue Riding Hood to herself.

So Blue Riding Hood carried on skipping to Wolf's house. Meanwhile Grandmother was at Wolf's house finishing off eating Wolf. "Yum, yum, that was delicious! Now all I need to do is dress in Wolf's clothes in case somebody comes," thought Grandmother to herself.

While Grandmother was getting dressed there was a knock on the door. "Who is it?" asked Grandmother, trying to sound like Wolf.

"It's Blue Riding Hood with some cakes for the party."

"Well come in."

Blue Riding Hood opened the sugar coated door and was surprised to find that Wolf didn't look like Wolf.

"My Wolf, what grey hair you have."

"All the better to keep me warm my friend."

"My Wolf, what evil red eyes you have."

"All the better to see you with my friend."

"My Wolf, you have no teeth."

"Wait a minute, can we cut this scene, I need to put my

teeth in… right carry on. All the better to eat you with my friend!"

"Ahhhhhhh," screamed Blue Riding Hood, running around the room, away from Grandmother of course.

"I've got you my pet," whispered Grandmother, ready to take a chunky bite out of Blue Riding Hood.

"Oh no you haven't," shouted a voice from the doorway.

"Who are you?" asked Grandmother and Blue Riding Hood together.

"I am Wizden the Grandmother slayer and you, Grandmother, shall die." And with one slash of Wizden's blade, Grandmother was split in two, leaving Wolf shocked and confused.

"Are you alright Wolf?" asked Blue Riding Hood, helping Wolf up.

"Oh no, the party is starting soon!"

"Don't worry, I invited everyone for you," said Wizden with a smile.

"Thank you so much," thanked Wolf.

"Guess what? They are all outside!" said Wizden, pointing outside to hundreds of people.

"Well, let them in," said Wolf with joy on his face. Wizden opened the door and hundreds of people went gushing in.

The party was a great success and the whole kingdom was invited (this included Rapunzel, Snow White, Rumplestiltskin and Sleeping Beauty). They all lived happily ever after (except for the Grandmother!).

Super Blue
by Thomas Dyson aged 9

Chapter One

Old Grandad Gurgle Glain was just an ordinary guy. He is 87 on 19th July. His height is 2 metres and his feet are 10 centimetres long. He lives on Gontly Avenue, No.9, on the right hand side of the road. Gontly Avenue is two blocks from the London Palace. It is a peaceful place really. The only noise you can really hear is barking dogs in number 65's back garden. Mrs Von Crocodile, who owns No.6 Gontly Avenue, loves dogs and owns 99 herself. She also owned a turtle, but paid no attention to it so it died of starvation. That's enough about starvation, lets get back to track.

If you have an old grandad like Mr Gurgle Glain, he would probably not be action packed, but Gurgle Glain was. Because his true identity is...

SUPER BLUE!

He fights evil and destroys every bad thing in sight.

Chapter Two

One fine morning on the 19th July (Gurgle Glain's birthday), lots of people were gathering at Grandad Gurgle Glain's front door step. Grandad Gurgle Glain was preparing a feast to eat. He was using herbs and tomato puree to create a birthday cake. Then after he had put the last drip of tomato puree on the top point of the cake, the Omerganoy TV screen came up. Gurgle Glain walked towards the TV screen but couldn't find the remote control. Gurgle Glain looked everywhere where the remote wasn't. Then he saw it. It was on top of the TV. Gurgle Glain reached for the remote. Because Gurlge Glain was so small, he couldn't reach the remote, so he went to get his stool from his bedroom. In a few minutes, Gurgle Glain came down with a tortoise sized stool. He ran over to the TV and placed the stool a few centimetres away from the screen. Gurgle Glain stood high on the small stool. The tiny stool made a big difference to his height. He grabbed the remote and pushed the stool aside. Gurgle Glain pressed the green button on the remote. This is what the TV said.

Super Blue, Help!

The Trobtic Arobit is attacking London.

Run to the palace and talk to King George VI.

Gurgle Glain ran upstairs as quick as a bullet and stepped into a black machine and, with a bang, boom, crash, Gurgle Glain turned into Super Blue!

Super Blue ran downstairs and opened the door for his friends.

"It's a fancy dress party folks," said Super Blue, rushing outside and getting into his Rocket Car 2000.

Super Blue started up the turbo engine and raced to the palace. Half way there, the police spotted Super Blue and chased him to the palace.

Chapter Three

The police were still on Super Blue's tail. Super Blue

was losing petrol. The police were shooting at him. "What could be worse?" shouted Super Blue. At that very moment it began to rain.

"Oh, boo-hoo," shouted Super Blue.

The next minute, Super Blue sighted the palace. He got out of his car and ran to the palace doors. The police stayed in their cars and drove after Super Blue. Super Blue got to the palace gates and tried to climb up. The police got out of their cars and got out pistols. Super Blue ran to the police and bashed the boss commander. The police got mad, so got into their cars. Super Blue had an easy entry to see King George VI.

Before Super Blue went through the gates of the palace, he went up to the knocked out police man and got his Luis Gun. Super Blue then squeezed through the gates of the castle and ran to the palace door. Two imperial guards ran up to him with dangerous looking axes. "Who are you?" shouted Guard One.

"I'm City Life Saver, Super Blue," yelled Super Blue.

"King George is expecting you," said Guard One.

"Pass," said Guard Two.

Super Blue ran in and was dazed by how much spiral stair cases there was.

"Hello, hello," said a voice from the top of the spiral stair case.

"Hello," said Super Blue, not knowing who was speaking.

"Hi," said King George, who was the unknown voice.

Super Blue told the King what had happened on his quest so far. Then the King told Super Blue what the rest of his quest would be. The King said, "Your next mission is to go to the city and destroy the evil giant spider Trobtic Arobit."

And with that, Super Blue raced outside, climbed through the gates and raced off in his Rocket Rally sport car. As soon as Super Blue got into his car, he saw the spider! So he got out again and loaded his Luis Gun. The spider was getting near and Super Blue was getting nervous. Super Blue shot the spider, but eventually saw he wasn't suffering so he picked up a discus. He swung the discus at the spider's head. The spider's head flew from its socket and the spider died instantly.

Super Blue was the hero of the world again, and he hasn't even had a proper challenge yet!

Haunted House Mystery
by Charlotte Hallam aged 11 years

It was a dark and gloomy night. Lesley and Martin woke up. "Martin, what are you doing?"

"Getting a glass of water," he replied. He went downstairs and, in the kitchen, he felt a draught run past him. "Ahhhh," screamed Lesley, jumping out of bed.

"What's wrong?" asked Martin.

"A shiver ran up my spine and it didn't feel nice."

Martin and Lesley went back to sleep.

The next day, Martin looked out of the window, the day was dim and gloomy. He went to make the bed, "Ahhh! Where is Lesley? She's gone!"

Meanwhile Lesley found herself away from home. "Why am I at my old school?"

Suddenly the lights turned off and then on again. The chalk board, which was on the desk, floated in mid-air and on it was written "GET OUT OF YOUR HOUSE NOW". Everything went dark and Lesley was back outside her house with the chalk board in her hand.

Martin came home. "Hi honey. I had a bad day at work," he moaned.

"Look at this, I found it in the old school," said Lesley.

"In your old school? Why were you there?" Lesley could not answer him.

It was getting dark. "What happened to you last night?" whispered Martin. Lesley was asleep so she didn't answer him.

The next day was dim and gloomy, the same as yesterday.

"Lesley's gone again!" shouted Martin. "That's two days in a row, what's happening?"

Three weeks later the spirit came to their house at night and wrote on their window. "THIS IS YOUR LAST WARNING. GET OUT OF YOUR HOUSE!"

Lesley heard a scratch. "What was….. hey, what's that?"

"THIS IS YOUR LAST WARNING, GET OUT OF YOUR HOUSE!" it said on the window.

"We've got to go," they both screamed.

The next day Lesley and Martin went to live at Lesley's mum's house in London. They came back to see their house a week after. "Wow, it's burnt down to a cinder," shouted Lesley.

"Do you believe we used to live there?" answered Martin. "I'm glad we listened to those letters, or we could have died."

In the end, Lesley and Martin saved up for a new house in London by getting new jobs. Martin started to believe in spirits.

The Night I Will Never Forget
by Amy Hanson aged 11

Chloe was lying in her bed when all of a sudden she heard the door move very slowly. "Who's there?" cried Chloe. There was something at the door that surprised her. There, at the door, was a figure. Its eyes were as black as the night sky, its skin was as white as a sheet and its hands looked as cold as ice.

"Please can I have a word with you?" asked a voice.

"Who are you?" replied Chloe.

"My name is Victoria Young," shouted the voice.

"OK, you may come in," Chloe said, feeling scared.

Victoria had a word with Chloe and Chloe found that Victoria had been murdered years ago, but the problem was her body was still in the house.

"How did you get murdered?" asked Chloe. "Did you get killed by accident?"

"Chloe, I didn't die by accident, my dad killed me!" Victoria responded.

Chloe's face went pale with shock. After a long conversation, Chloe fell asleep and woke up at 12.00am. Chloe was determined to tell the police about Victoria and how she had died. So she did. At first the police didn't believe her, but when she took them to her house everything changed. They ripped up the floorboards and found Victoria's body near the chimney in Chloe's room.

The police found the evidence they needed about the murder and were able to close the case. Victoria's body was buried.

That night, Victoria came to see Chloe for the very last time. She said to Chloe, "Thank you for helping me, I will now be able to rest in peace. I will not be troubling you again."

"You're welcome and goodbye," replied Chloe.

Chloe watched Victoria vanish and, as Victoria went, a star glistened in the sky. Chloe's day was over and so she fell asleep and dreamt about her unusual day.

A Strange Happening
by Jacob Jennings aged 10

"Fine then!" bellowed Tom's Aunt Bettie. "Burn the stupid sofa!"

Tom's Uncle Fred was trying to reason with his wife. "Look dear, I promised Tom we would burn it and it's getting old. Oh, and try not to wake Tom, he's only just gone to sleep."

"We'll continue this in the morning Frederick! I'm off to bed – coming?"

When they had gone to bed, the living room door creaked open and footsteps echoed along the landing.

Tom woke to a cold wind, he turned over and looked at his alarm clock, it said 1.00 am. When Tom sat up he saw the shadow of a tall boy, probably around 11 years old. In a weak and feeble voice Tom said, "Who are you?"

"I, I am Robbie. I lived in this house in the 1900s. You must not burn the sofa." Then he vanished.

It was 8.00 am. Aunt Bettie was cooking breakfast and Tom said to her, "Last night I was visited by a ghost. He said he was called Robbie."

"Now Tom, you know it was only a dream."

"But Aunt, he said not to burn the sofa."

Footsteps came down the stairs, big heavy footsteps. "That's him," Tom said. It was only Uncle Fred. "We're going to the zoo today. We'll go after we've finished breakfast."

It was late when they got home. As soon as they got home Tom went up to bed. Again Tom woke to a cold wind at 1.00 am. Tom sat up and, sure enough, Robbie was sitting on his windowsill. "Hello again," he said. "Follow me." He wafted out of the room and down the stairs like a puff of smoke. Robbie drifted over to the sofa and told Tom to lift up the left sofa cushion. "Push where I am pointing," Robbie ordered. Tom did as he was told, pushed and a crinkly noise went through the room. "What is it?"

"That," said Robbie, "that is the document that I hid for my great, great, great grandchild to find with my help. In the morning, give it to your Aunt or Uncle."

"OK, I'm going back to bed."

In the morning, Tom rushed downstairs and told Aunt Bettie what he had found. Aunt Bettie took a knife from the drawer and slit the lining of the sofa. She called her husband, "Fred, look what I've got."

"What is it?" he asked.

"It's a document that will end all our troubles. It says we own all this land. We can sell the land and get out of the tiny house. After breakfast we'll sell the land at the Estate Agent and look for a new house at the same time." So that's what they did.

Three weeks later, Tom, Aunt Bettie and Uncle Fred were moving their furniture into a larger house. That was the last Tom ever saw of Robbie. But without him they would be living in a council house now.

The Curse Of The Dragon
by Dimitri Kitromilides aged 10

As Thomas steadily approached the cave, he heard the roar once again but louder. When Thomas moved, everything became clearer, the tree's branches looked like arms reaching out to grab you and the cave looked as dark and dull as a pitch black night. Thomas was just about to enter the cave and it came again. He jumped out of his skin. Then in the darkness, Thomas could see a light shadow on the wall, it was getting faster and it was increasing in size. Suddenly, flying at Thomas at over 50 mph was a huge fire-breathing dragon! Thomas dived to the ground, the dragon just swooped above Thomas, he had a narrow escape.

As Thomas watched the dragon, it soared up into the mountains. As it expanded its wings to its full wingspan, it looked gigantic. Thomas was puzzled. What kind of place was this, wicked trees, spooky caves and now dragons, what next ? Thomas decided to explore the cave. It was full of debris and weeds, the more he moved the darker it got, but to Thomas's surprise he saw light. He rushed to see what was there. All Thomas could see were flames. In the corner of his eye, he could see a figure wailing for help. Thomas suspected that the dragon had set the cave to flames. Thomas rushed through the flames, being careful not to burn himself. When Thomas got to the injured person, he himself was in worse shape. He and the person stood up and started sprinting for the entrance. Thomas saw a peek of light from the cave entrance. That was the good news, but the bad news was the fire was gaining. He could now properly see the entrance and he was moving at some pace, but so was the fire. Thomas dived for the entrance, but the fire caught his pants, he barely made it out. He sprinted for the little pool, he shot his leg into the pool. His grey pants and white trainers were ruined. Luckily, it didn't catch his black and white sweater. He looked at his pants, burnt to a crisp and black but soaking wet. Thomas approached the figure with caution, he slowly removed the hood and saw a young girl with long blonde hair down to her shoulders and bright blue eyes, in fact she looked no older than Thomas. She regained consciousness and slowly climbed to her feet. Thomas didn't know where he was, he was completely lost, he asked the girl if she knew where they were. She replied that she knew where they were loosely. Thomas thought it was rude not to call her by her name, so he asked her. She replied, "Mary." Thomas had never seen a place like this before, as he moved it got harder for him to see where he was. There was a fog surrounding them, he was being led up into the mountains.

"Are you sure you know where we're going?" asked Thomas, sounding worried.

"Of course I know where I'm going, there's an abandoned port on the other side of the island, but to get there we have to go through the mountains where the dragon lives."

At that second, the dragon appeared at the top of the mountain and hit a large stone boulder in Thomas and Mary's direction. It hit a number of other boulders and started a landslide. It knocked Thomas and Mary off their feet and down the hillside. When he awoke he opened his eyes, but to be staring into complete darkness. Mary was already exploring the small, cramped room. Thomas got up to find a way out. He saw a hole of light, small but big enough to crawl through. He pushed and gradually got out. Then he helped Mary out, with a hard tug she got through. Then Thomas could see a little wooden dock in the distance, it would be a struggle, he would make it, he had to make it. It was getting dark so they both decided to camp. Thomas reassured Mary they'd both get there tomorrow. In the morning, once again, Mary woke up before Thomas. Thomas remembered he found those two parachutes in the attic, he jumped up and darted for his rucksack. He opened it and, to his relief, they were in there. He grabbed them and gave one to Mary. Thomas had never parachuted before, he was planning to practice but he never did, he had other things on his hands. Thomas strapped the parachutes on and jumped, he had the pleasure of flying so high and not being worried. He had a perfect landing, so did Mary, but the dragon had beat them there. The dragon bit at the parachute and ripped them in half. Thomas ran to the ships. He dived into a ship as Mary followed him. To Thomas's surprise, it was a pirate ship. He saw a beautiful silver sword gleaming in the sunlight. He reached out for the sword but the dragon was once again coming at him. A position Thomas never wished to be in again. Thomas swung the sword with all his might and cleanly cut the dragon's head off. Thomas watched the dragon as all its movement stopped – it was never to move again.

The Dragon's Valley
by Dominic Liffen aged 10

As Figo crept towards the cave he heard crying from within. He forgot his fears and went into the cave, listening for the crying. He followed the crying into the very heart of the cave, where, on a large marble stone sat... nothing!

He suddenly turned to see the door close. He cried out and ran towards the door, beating his fists against it. He soon realised the door was as solid as oak. Turning round he saw a ladder hanging from the ceiling. He sprinted towards it, tripping over the marble stone in his haste to get to the ladder. He jumped up and grasped the ladder with his sweaty hands. The rungs seemed to take an eternity to climb thought Figo. When he got to the top he knew why. He had emerged on top of the mountain! He knew this because he nearly walked off the edge of the cliff himself. He looked around for a way down despairingly for a few moments. Then he spotted a narrow path leading down to the valley. He charged down the path, heedless to the avalanche he was causing. Just before he reached the bottom, a stray rock fell from overhead, causing him to lose consciousness.

When Figo came round he was lying on the ground by the waterfall. Unsteadily, he got to his feet and walked around, trying to find his balance like a new born calf. Before he could though, the ground gave way and Figo fell through the air, screaming himself hoarse. He landed on his back, knocking the wind out of him. He lay in the dark for a few moments, trying to get his breath back. Eventually, he stood up and lit a candle with a match he had in his backpack. With the small flame he could see a door painted blue. Without taking any chances, he shoulder-barged the door, bursting into an extremely bright light. "Owww," screamed Figo as the searing bright light forced him to his knees. Then, as it passed, he stood moaning, "My eyes, my eyes." He rubbed his eyes and adjusted his eyes to the gloom. Finally, he saw what had made the light. A dragon! It was chained up, spurting orange, white and blue flames at him. He dodged and picked up a sword he had seen lying against the wall. He swung it around to see if he could lift it. It was surprisingly light he thought. The sword seemed to be encrusted with diamonds and rubies. He ran towards the dragon, silently dodging the dancing flames of fire. The dragon had spotted Figo a little too late. Figo cut its head off with one chop. He stood panting, staring into the glassy eyes of the dragon closing in a deep and eternal sleep.

The Beetle
by Nick Brown aged 8

As my eyes fell on the dark mouth of the cave, I only just realised what I was looking at. The sheer size of the cave made my mouth drop and my eyes bulge. The cave was as dark as a black hole. I couldn't see a thing. I went in because there was nowhere else to go.

That was when I heard a loud scuttling sound. I felt a movement at my feet. I knelt down and picked up a small creature. It was a beetle. I walked back out of the cave and into the night. Then I saw the beetle's true form. It was splodged with multi-coloured spots. I held the beetle close to my eye to examine it. It kicked me. It scratched my nose. I squeezed it. It bit me. It put some sort of drug in me. I suddenly felt sleepy. I fell to the ground and slept. In the morning, I woke up because the beetle was crawling across my stomach. My finger still hurt. I looked at it. The skin was as clear as crystal. I could see all of the tendons and the bones moving. I was very shocked. I screamed, I decided to go for a walk to calm myself down. I pulled my gloves on. Then I remembered about the beetle. I wanted to eat it, but I was scared that the beetle would bite my tongue. That beetle was a mean, mini Hitler. I had found on the walk a water-fall with a pond at the bottom and the water was as clear as glass. The water had been overflowing the pond. I wondered where all the water went. My eyes followed the water until it fell down a big crack in the ground. Then I went back to the mouth of the cave. Suddenly, I felt a small movement in my trouser pocket. Something small fell out of it and scuttled over my feet. It must of crawled into my pocket when I fell asleep (I decided to call my beetle Hitler). I took my gloves off because they were getting sweaty. Then I saw my worst nightmare, my whole hand had disease from Hitler. I pulled my gloves back on. I couldn't bear to see my hand in such a horrible condition. Soon after, my whole hand had the horrendous disease. My head swam. I was too creeped out to even hurt the beetle. I thought of horrid thoughts. What would my family say when they saw my arm. It was a too horrible thought to even scream. I ripped at my hair and kicked walls. Then I remembered the waterfall. It would calm me down. I thought about it, then I went. I stripped and got in. I forgot about every bad thing and I liked it a lot. I didn't even feel the beetle biting me. I woke up because I heard a noise. I looked at my skin. It was normal, I got out of the water and stood on Hitler. Then I heard loud scuttling again. I looked and saw a whole army of beetles. Hitler was their father. I got back in the pool. The beetles surrounded me. I cried for help. None came. I decided to make a run for it. It was the only way. I climbed out and ran, I am still running 3 years after and I still keep going. I've learned never to go into caves ever again.

Snifferella
by Lucy Smith aged 9

One pleasant summer's day, Snifferella was munching on a lovely patch of green, juicy grass when something brown caught her eye.

Snifferella was a beautiful white, black and brown rabbit. She had a black eye and a brown eye and lovely long brown ears.

The thing that caught her eye was another brown wild rabbit. His name was Barry. The moment their eyes met they fell deeply in love. They played all day long and hunted for food at night.

On March the 1st, when the sun was just setting, Barry proposed, and can you guess what Snifferella said? She said yes.

So the very next day they were married. Everyone came. Thursday the duck and her boyfriend, the two female pheasants and Pheas, the male pheasant, Mr and Mrs Dove, Mr and Mrs Woodpecker. In fact, all the animals in Old Glossop came and for confetti they used blossom petals. All was a success and everyone lived happily ever after.

At The Zoo
by Niamh Foley aged 6

One day a girl and a boy went to the zoo. When they got there they went to see the elephants. They saw a mummy elephant, a daddy elephant and a baby elephant. The mummy and daddy elephants were washing the baby elephant.

After that they went to see the giraffes. The giraffes were eating from tall trees. They had brown spots on their yellow body and they also had very long necks.

The boy and girl were now hungry so they went to a café for some lunch. The girl had ham sandwiches and the boy had cheese sandwiches. They were very nice.

After dinner they went to see the lions. The lions were big and scary and had very sharp teeth. The zoo-keeper came to feed the lions, he gave them lots of meat to eat.

Now the boy and girl were very tired so they went home to bed. They had a lovely time at the zoo.

Chestnut
by Amy Smith aged 8

There once lived a lucky little girl named Angela. Her father was very rich and they lived in a beautiful house in the country. Angela's father owned a factory and a big field outside his house. Angela's pride and joy was a strong stallion called Chestnut. One misty evening, Angela's father came home rather upset.

"I'm so sorry Angela," he mumbled, "my factory has to close down."

"Oh father," said Angela.

"Wait, I've not finished. This bit is worst of all. We have to sell Chestnut."

"CHESTNUT!" cried Angela. "You can't."

"I'm sorry dear, we have to."

The day came for Angela to say her last goodbye to Chestnut. A spoilt little boy came and bought Chestnut. "Mother," he yelled. "I don't want it to be called Chestnut, I want to change his name NOW!"

"Bye Chestnut."

"He's not called Chestnut any more," screamed the little boy.

"Father, will I ever see Chestnut again?" asked Angela.

"I'm afraid not," replied her father.

"I will come with the money next Wednesday," said the naughty boy's mother.

Then on Tuesday night, the day before Chestnut should have been sold, a man came and said, "I want to buy the factory and it will be a reasonable offer." Angela's father took up the offer and said, "We don't have to sell Chestnut any more," and rang up the naughty boy to tell him. Angela was overjoyed.

Classroom Horror
by Amanda Jones aged 11

It was a normal day at school for Clarie and Sophie, usually they came to school, put their bags down and sat down to work, but not today. Clarie walked into the classroom to see Mrs Sleg, their teacher, wasn't there. Instead it was a supply teacher, Miss Terror. By the look of her face she was a terror.

Clarie sat down, got out her books and wrote her spellings down, then Mrs Blackmore came in with a note saying Sophie was ill but Sophie was never ill. Clarie was worried. All of a sudden the door slammed shut and the blinds flew down.

"Right, today is not like any of your other days. Today is a special day."

All the boys were laughing but not for long, Miss Terror slammed a book down, the boys jumped and stopped laughing. Miss Terror's eyes were going yellow, black was growing on her hair and her nails grew as long as a brand new rubber. Then the lights went dim and Miss Terror grabbed Shaun and threw him to the other end of the classroom. Everyone screamed, Shaun was covered in cuts.

"Now sit down!"

Clarie realised why the blinds were down, the lights were dim. Miss Terror, or the creature, could not stand the sunlight, that's why her car windows were sun-free. Clarie told Shaun to throw a rubber.

"No way," he refused.

"Is there talking?"

It all happened again, but this time Clarie and Rachel and Jess ran around the class, lifting up the blinds. Miss Terror screamed and turned to dust. At that second Miss Sleg ran in, "Are you OK?"

"Yes, we are so glad you are back," and they told Miss Sleg the whole story.

The War Of The Worlds: They're Already Here!
by Melissa Bowker aged 10

It was a normal Sunday night on Rovers Avenue. Everyone was just their ordinary selves. Children finishing hot chocolates and slumping into their warm beds, with their parents sipping their cups of fruit tea with the TV control in the other hand.

The Jones family was just crawling up their hill-like stairs, trying not to fall asleep until they got to their beds. Mr Jones was tucking the children into bed while Mrs Jones was drawing the curtains, but suddenly she saw colourful flashing lights in the distance. At first she thought it was nothing important, for she remembered there was a concert in the town centre, but then the lights started to get brighter and brighter. Surely they can't be concert lights now for they were too bright?

She told Mr Jones and curious he was. He got everyone up again and took them outside. By this time there were strange noises too and nearly all of Rovers

Avenue were outside, huddled up to their families for comfort. Nobody was talking for they were too curious to even ask a neighbour what was going on. The noises started to get louder and the louder they got the more the families huddled.

Then suddenly a big blue light started to get bigger and bigger until it started to get closer and closer and quicker and quicker until BOOM! It struck the earth, shaking and terrorising all of Rovers Avenue. It destroyed the Jones' house and a lot more, cars were destroyed and families were separated (even the annoying dog that had lived next door to the Jones family was destroyed). Then there appeared, out of the smoke and debris, a giant magnetic monster. Each time its magnificent metal, razor sharp claws hit the ground, it dug into anything it hit and shook all of Rovers Avenue. Its luminous green eyes were so bright they lit the sky and terrified everyone. Its stilt-like legs strode over all the houses that remained. What were they going to do? Who would save them? Mr and Mrs Jones were looking for their children when Mr Jones saw Becky, his 19 year old daughter, climbing one of the magnetic monsters. Mr Jones went running after her because he knew shouting was no good. The sounds of screaming and destroying would drown out his voice easily, then he heard a faint sound from behind him. It was his wife calling him.

"Tom, Tom, what are you doing? I thought we were

supposed to be looking for the children."

Mr Jones called back, while dodging the laser beams, "I've found Becky."

Mrs Jones didn't realise her daughter was in trouble so she just shouted back to her husband (although because he was so far away he couldn't hear her) that she would stay in her hiding place and wait for their son.

Mr Jones caught up with Becky and tried to persuade her to come down, but she kept resisting and said with a brave voice, "No! No! I'm not going back until all of us are safe. I've already lost my brother so I'm not going to lose anyone else." In the end Mr Jones gave up.

"All right then, but I will help."

Becky told her dad about a book she had read in college and what it said on how to defeat any alien. "All it said was to shout "Love" at it and it will be destroyed, because, you see, aliens weren't brought up to give peace like us humans do, so it would kill them."

Her dad was confused but agreed to help. As they got to the top of the monster robot, Becky told her dad the plan. "I know it sounds dangerous and risky, but if you can distract the alien in there long enough for me to get to the speakers and say my lines, it would destroy all of the aliens here." So that's what they did.

Mr Jones jumped into the room and strangled the alien long enough for Becky to do her lines and it worked. She shouted at the top of her voice, "LOVE."

Mr Jones was no longer strangling any alien but found black dust where the alien had been and laughed while hugging Becky, "Its over, its over!" he said and cried.

Beware!
by Rachel Barber aged 11

Emma and Jade were walking down the very busy school hallway. Then all the noisy, loud children disappeared and they were the only people there, but break had just started. They looked around the school, but no children, teachers or cleaners were there. Suddenly they heard bounce, bounce, bounce. They turned around and walked in the sports hall; no-one was there, but a ball bouncing around the hall. The ball rolled to Emma and Jade's feet with a note attached. They ran home and the note fell to the floor. The children's teachers and cleaners appeared and the day continued.

The next day Emma and Jade were playing out, Emma's bike started riding up and down the street and wrote on the floor the exact same thing as the note. "Beware! Beware!" A face appeared on the bike. A white, pasty face and brown fading eyes stared at them. The bike came back to Emma and the ghost disappeared. Emma and Jade looked at each other and ran away.

At school lots of weird things kept happening, like books floating that only they could see, or people's hats floating off their heads. Everything that happened managed to have a way of writing "Beware! Beware!" After school, walking back home, each of them heard a windy misty voice saying, "Beware, beware!" Suddenly there was a bang. "Did you hear that?" mumbled Jade. "Bang! Bang! Bang!" Everything went black and they couldn't see anything. Both of them fell to the floor and the light turned back on and the pasty face appeared and said, "I told you to beware!" Emma and Jade just lay there on the floor until a search party looked over the girls and they sat up weakly. "What happened, what happened?" their mums and dads said. "I don't know, I don't know," replied Emma and Jade. The police tried to solve what had happened with the information they'd given, but they couldn't.

Silent As The Grave
by Jamie Cowle aged 10

It was a cool crisp night on the A47, perfect for young drivers like John to speed along on the wide open road. Suddenly, out of thin air, a woman appeared on the edge of the road next to Box Hill Wood. John slowed down expertly and then came to a stop next to the woman. He asked if she wanted a ride home, the woman nodded slowly and opened the door with her long pale arms. Almost instantly an eerie chill trickled its way down John's spine.

The woman didn't say anything for the first few

minutes, John was getting to feel a bit spooked out so he tried to engage her in conversation.

"So what's your name then miss?" he asked in the kindest voice he could manage. The woman remained silent, this scared John more than ever, it was like he wasn't there. It was then strange and eerie things started to happen, the window next to where the woman was sitting started to frost over. Her fingers seemed to make a cracking sound and slide themselves into angles that any human thought was impossible. But what made John most scared was that, while her fingers continuously kept breaking and the temperature in the car was permanently dropping, she sat there and just plaited her beautifully long blonde hair without pausing once to say, "Ow!" or wince in the slightest way, shape or form.

Then the woman signalled to stop the car. So, being a little more cautious this time, John slowly stopped, almost forgetting to switch the gears.

The woman stepped out of the car, opening the door with her one and only unbroken finger. All of a sudden the frost on the window, the smell and the eerie chill, all disappeared. Only one thing was left behind, her golden brown bearskin coat. So, reluctantly, John, only thinking it was polite, took the shiny fur coat to the front door of the small cottage he saw the strange woman go into. To his surprise an old woman opened the door, she spoke in a high cheery voice, but there was a sadness and despair in her eyes. "Can I help you?"

"I think your daughter has left her coat in my car," John replied, still a bit befuddled about the very weird woman. But instead of saying thank you and taking the coat, the woman said in the same fake cheery voice. "There must be some mistake, that is impossible, my daughter crashed her car on the A47 exactly five years ago today. She was thrown through the window of the car and was found hanging from a tree in Box Hill Wood. All of her fingers had been broken and her coat was never found." With that she let out a sob and took a small picture out from a pocket in her cardigan and turned it to John. The picture was of the pretty woman who had been sitting in John's car only seconds ago. John's eyes bulged, he turned pale white and fainted on the spot.

Charlie
by Jocelyn Woodhouse aged 10

Charlie had just finished school for the summer hols. She threw her bags in the corner and was just about to shout her mum when Charlie's mum shouted her. That NEVER happens.

"Mum!! Where are you?" Charlie yelled through the house as she walked upstairs to get out of her boring school uniform.

Charlie was 13 and her real name was Charlotte, but

all her friends call her Charlie. She was into skateboarding, baggy clothes, everything most girls wouldn't dream of doing.

"I'm in the kitchen," her mother replied. When Charlie was changed she ran downstairs to greet her mum. Her mother was smiling strangely, as if she was dazed.

"What's up with you?" Charlie asked. Her mum didn't make eye contact. "Nothing," she replied, staring practically straight through Charlie, as if trying to read something on the wall.

"Whatever. I'm going out," Charlie said as she went to get her skateboard.

"OK dear, bye." Her mum was still staring at the wall. That was strange, Charlie's mum would usually enquire about where she was going. Something was definitely wrong. She turned around and went back home and crouched in front of the kitchen window. Her mother had moved now, but Charlie couldn't understand. There was a beam of light coming from the ceiling and her mum was walking into it. She floated up through the ceiling into the sky. Concerned for her mother, Charlie leapt through the open window into the light. She floated up behind her mother and nobody ever saw them again.

The Italian Ghost
by Ella Newton aged 8

"Carly! We've got to go down to the breakfast hall. And, yes, you can take your book before you ask," shouted mum. Carly was mad about reading. You could never see her without a book in her hand, reading the latest Beano or a big bag full of children's novels. Her father was a pig and was always choosing the biggest and most expensive meal. Her mother was exactly the opposite. She chose salad usually and other light meals. She had a whole room at home full of make-up, lipstick and nail varnish.

As Carly came down the stairs, clutching Charlie and the Chocolate Factory by Roald Dahl, her father put on his dining suit. They set off down the maze of twisting corridors. As Carly was reading and her mother and father were talking about last night's football, they went off in different directions. Carly looked up from her book, because she'd finished it, and found herself in a strange room.

It was a small, stuffy room, full of shelves with magical objects, such as lots of pots with multi-coloured potions inside, bubbling with anger, a transparent box about the size of a child's head, which was full of golden stars floating in a silvery liquid, a set of an old oak wand, hat and cloak. The hat and cloak were patterned purple with silver moons and stars. On top of the dustiest shelf was an old padlocked spell book and standing on it was a phoenix with a collar saying, "Fireball", staring at a crystal ball.

"Oh no, I've lost mum and dad," shouted Carly.

"Ello, ello. Who iz thees? I am Enzo Magico."

"Aarrghh! Oooh I'm Carly."

Enzo was the castle ghost and was born in Italy. Before he died he did fantastic magic performances.

"Can you help m-me g-get out of here? P-please," stammered Carly.

"No. I aam going to kip you here forever!"

"K-krreek," cawed Fireball, heading towards the door with the rusty lock and started pecking at it with his strong beak.

"No! No! No!" Enzo was getting weaker without his phoenix. Eventually he vanished into thin air. By that time the phoenix flew outside and underground. There, he made dents in the floor from Carly to her mother and father.

"CARLY," squawked the phoenix.

Her mother and father were so busy talking they didn't realise that Carly had gone. They were very hungry by then and ate ravenously. When Carly got back to her room she was surprised to find a phoenix statue with a Fireball collar.

"So it did happen!" she thought.

Adventure On Dino Island
by Liza Vul aged 7

It all began in school, my dad picked me up early for some reason. He said we had to catch a train to the 2.00 p.m. boat to Australia, to tell you the truth my dad's a scientist, he was going to Australia to study Ayers Rock and taking me to be his assistant, but on the way a terrible storm blew over the boat. It rocked side to side so much that the captain managed to slip and knock himself out! We all went in our cabins and snuggled deep down in our beds, waiting for the boat to stop rocking and the sound of thunder to stop roaring. In the morning we opened the door and found we were not on salty water. We were swiped on a shore of sand and shells.

"This is not Australia, this is a jungle!" shouted my dad.

Just a moment later a giant "ROAR" echoed through our ears. An enormous green dinosaur ran out of the trees to crash the boat. Luckily, most of the crew managed to jump off board and swim quite far from the murderous creature. Then we swam to the other side of the island and walked through the jungle night and day, night and day.

"I can't go on any more," I groaned.

"Sshh, I can hear something, follow me everyone," whispered my dad. We followed him and after a minute or two he stopped, so did we. To our great surprise we saw a village. People greeted us and took us in a tent and gave us food and water.

"Greetings visitors. I am Elma the great chief of the village. We are planning to train dinosaurs and put them in shows. As you see, we are all very busy getting ready and building the festival roundabout and helter-skelter. You can help tomorrow. Right now, you must rest from your long journey. Just then a roar, just like the first one, drew close. Everyone ran into a tent, no matter if it was theirs or not. Everyone zipped up the little entrance in their tent, hoping that they would not be the cannibal's dinner. He passed the first tent and then he passed the second and third, fourth, fifth, sixth, seventh and then he stopped in front of ours. She could possibly hear us breathe, for we had forgot to close the back entrance.

"Dad, I need to sneeze," I whispered.

"Don't you dare," he whispered back.

My dad sneaked up to the back of the tent and started to carefully zip up the back entrance. He was halfway through it when I started sniffing. "A, A, A, A, A, Achoooo!"

My dad finished just in time. The dinosaur stomped off, thinking it was just another empty old tent. After one or two minutes later, everyone came out, positive they were safe.

"Do you see why we have to be so careful?" said Elma.

"Yes," I panted.

97

The next morning, I shot up out of my bed like a rocket. I ran straight outside to find my dad waiting at the side of the tent. "Good morning," he said with a bit of rhythm in it. He had a tray of buns in his left hand, in the right hand he held a teapot. He sat down in the tent and gave me a bun, then he poured some tea in a cup and put it in my hand. After that I skipped out to meet Elma.

"Hello," he smiled. "There is work to be done. You see those men over there, they are chopping wood up, go and take it over to the helter-skelter would you?" he asked me. I went to work straight away, whilst my dad was trying to make sure the roundabout was stable. After a long day's work I seemed to be quite proud of myself, my dad was too. After one or two months, me and my dad took a day off because Elma said he would try and get us on a boat back to England, so we were getting ready, and finally we got there.

I passed the story on to my children, they shall pass it on to theirs and on and on, for it was the greatest adventure ever.

A Journey Through Time
by Megan Hillier aged 8

Once, in a dark and gloomy wood, lived a creature that had never been seen in all history. It had horns as sharp as razors and its eyes were like steaming flames of fire. It had friends that came out with him at night and danced unusual dances until the sun shone above them. Then they would climb up a tree and doze off to sleep. In the morning they would admire the sites beyond them and go hunting for skunks and rabbits and all other animals. Now this was in the early 19th Century. The story really begins now. It was 2005, the birds were singing, the boats were sailing and the wind was whistling, but most of all, and this is quite strange, when I was walking I saw a dog but it was blue! And I saw a cat that was green! I stopped for a minute and thought, then I rushed home and turned on the TV. "Phew!" I said to myself, the news was still on. I sat and watched in amazement. I decided to go and call for my friend and told mum and dad and went out the door to Anna's. I rang the door bell and she opened the door. "I must talk to you," I bellowed.

"Come in, come in," said Anna. "Now, what did you want to say?"

"Well, I was watching the news and there was lots of different coloured animals, like pink cats and purple dogs." I said, "I want to look for the thing that's causing it. Yes, let us go to the shop and buy some food and equipment."

"OK," said Anna. "Bye Mum, bye Dad."

When we had been to the shop they ran through the street so they wouldn't be seen and finally they came to a forest.

"It's chilly in here isn't it?" I said.

Soon we came to something very mysterious. It was a time machine! There was a label on it saying *Time Machine – Do Not Touch.*

"What's that snoring noise?" said Anna.

"I don't know," I replied.

Anna went and looked in the window of the time machine, being careful that she didn't touch it. "Oh oh!"

"What did you see?" I said.

"I saw some kind of creature. It had horns and big eyes."

"What? What is it?" I shouted.

"Don't be so loud," said Anna to me.

"It's too late," said Anna. "We've woken it up, something came out of the time machine."

"HELP!" shouted both of us at the same time.

"Run!" shouted Anna.

Suddenly something said, "It's alright, I won't hurt you."

We looked around and saw a monster.

"Are you friendly?" I said.

"Of course I am."

"Oh," we said. "What's your name?"

"My name is Tinkastick," it said.

"Well Tinkastick, tell us what you have done."

"Well, a long time ago I wanted to go to sleep, but I couldn't find anywhere, so I just found a patch of mud and went to sleep, but then it started to snow and I got snowed over. Nearby a group of scientists were working and they got hold of me, but they were supposed to get some snow. They put me in their time machine so it would stand up, but it didn't, so one of the scientists pressed all the buttons, so I went flying off to 2005. That's how I got here. I don't know how to get anywhere."

"We'll help you and I'll make you a new house."

So we got twigs and leaves and made a house.

"Wait Tinkastick, do you know anything about the different colour animals?" I said.

"Yes I did."

"Well, we must be going, bye."

Well, there's another happy ending.

The Five Girls And The Swimming Pool
by Anna Tuckwell aged 8

There once lived three girls called Charlotte, Katie and Lizzie. They lived in Australia in one big spooky house. They went to school that morning because it was Thursday. Charlotte, Katie and Lizzie and the rest of their class went swimming. Katie was in the deep end and the other two girls were in the shallow end. Katie was practising her diving. She had a spotty costume on and blue goggles. Lizzie and Charlotte were practising breast-stroke and Katie was under the water when she saw a big green tunnel.

"Aaahhh!" screamed Katie. "I'm never ever coming to

this swimming pool again!"

"Katie, wait, what's wrong?" said Lizzie and Charlotte.

"I'm getting dressed straight away and going home, in my bedroom I'm going to do something." What was she going to do?

"Me and Charlotte will carry on doing our breast-stroke. Just leave her, she is just being silly."

"Oh no she isn't, but what is the problem?"

"She has seen our secret. Years ago we wanted Australia not hot anymore but cold and wet, so we connected a tunnel to the swimming pool, and behind the curtain there is a switch. It switches the bubble machine on, that makes the water flood all over Australia."

That moment, Katie came out of the middle of nowhere. "I'm going down that tunnel and I'm going to investigate."

"No wait, there is a big salty ocean down there, you will get lost if you go down there, it is not a good idea, please don't."

She got her swimming costume and dived down.

"Noooo! My best friend has gone now because of you two, I'm going to ring the police. 999! I am going to save Katie."

Katie whispered, "This is great without my friends and family. Well, not really without my friends and family, but it's more quiet and more musical.

Musical? I hear music." She swam over. There was a man and a lady dancing, there were people swimming.

"Hello. I'm Sam." "And I'm Samantha, but they all call me Sammy. We used to be your teachers and saw the tunnel as well."

"I am missing my friends and family. I am going to go back to the swimming pool." She swam and swam and swam. Finally she got back to the tunnel. "Lizzie, Charlotte, I'm never going to leave you again. Shall we go to the house and go to bed?"

"Yes, sure."

The Goblin's Revenge
by Ollie Barnard aged 10

After three long, hard hours of knitting a small coat for his grandson, Rodger sighed and walked over to the window. He was thinking about the pixies. "Nasty little, screeching things!" he muttered to himself quietly, for Leila, his daughter, was asleep. It was obviously not nearly quiet enough though, as Leila awoke with a start.

"Err? Father?"

"Oh, sorry to wake you darling. I was just thinking about the pixies." Leila sat up in bed.

"I just want revenge!" Rodger cried.

"I, King Goblin of Mower Hall, Rodger Yout, will not let the pixies of Merrad Tower steal ALL my treasure and get away with it!!!"

His green skin crumpled up and his pointed ears stuck on end.

"Father, father! Calm down! Shouting will not make any difference at all!"

Half an hour later, all the residents of Mower Hall were sitting in the hall eating breakfast. Roast beef was on the menu (unfortunately, not one of Rodger's favourites).

"I hope you all like it!" the cook declared. She spoke with an Irish accent.

"Yes...," Rodger replied thoughtfully. "I've been thinking."

"You have?" Jake, one of the younger goblins looked up at him cheekily.

"Ermm.... It's about those pixies. There is NO way they're going to get away with this! And so he began to explain his great plan to every one of the forty-three goblins sitting around the table.

On that same day, at the dead of night, Percy crept out of the main doors. Merrad Tower was just over the hill, about a twenty minute walk (for a goblin that it is; for you or me it would take about an hour!). Percy was not alone though. Robert and Henry were right behind him. Hurriedly, but as quietly as a mouse, the three goblins made their way across the hill, until they finally reached Merrad Tower. Robert gasped, "It's taller than I remembered!" he gaped. "And I remember it to be jolly tall!" Only Henry could see the top of the tower, as he was older, wiser and had far better eyesight than the other two.

"Ok," he began, and took a breath before he continued. "We must distract the guards so Rodger can creep in behind them."

"Yes, but how exactly?" Percy asked.

"I don't know! Just shout something." Robert was enjoying this.

"You who!" he shouted, sounding just like Rodger's wife – Alicia. Immediately, the guards turned their heads and peered into the darkness.

"Who's out there?" one of them squeaked.

"How should I know!" Percy called.

"Hey!" one of them called inquisitively.

"We're coming to get you!" the others shouted.

"Are you?" Henry asked from the darkness. Quickly, the guards exchanged glances and then ran into the night, hoping they would bump into whoever was calling out to them (they didn't though).

Rodger, who had been hiding behind the side of the building all this time, sprinted off into the tower and looked around. Ahead of him was a large tunnel, slowly going up. To his left was another tunnel, smaller than the other and going down instead of up. Finally, on his right was a plain wall with a picture of the King Pixie – King Flosindell. Rodger knew vaguely where the treasure would be, so he took the smaller tunnel on the left. The walls were lit by candlelight, which gave Rodger a sparkling yellow glow to see his way round. Hundreds of tunnels cut off at the sides, but Rodger kept walking and walking and walking. Finally he came to his destination. A barred gate in the middle of the tunnel. On the other side of the gate he could see a windowsill. So, with a heave, he pushed his big, hairy, wrinkled arm through one of the holes in the gate and reached over to the sill. For a few seconds he stood there fumbling around until he found it. The key! He knew it was there, for back in Mower Hall they had a picture of Flosindell and, in the background, there was a barred gate and, next to the gate, there was a window and you can probably guess what was on the windowsill. The key! Rodger breathed a sigh of relief but, as he did so, dropped the key.

"Oh no," he moaned. Sweat began to trickle down his arms as he reached down to the floor and tried to grab they key. It was no use, it was just too far away. He looked around but could only see bare walls. Bare walls… that gave him an idea. Hurriedly, he scraped against the walls, the mud falling into his hands. Seconds later, he found what he was looking for – a root. With one great pull, he managed to get a good chunk out. Carefully, he straightened it out and then held the tip of it in his hand. Again, he pushed his hand through a gap between the bars and reached out to the key. He had used the root to extend his finger and luckily it was a nice thick, strong root, so he was able to slide the key out with no problem. Then, he slid it into the keyhole and pushed. The door immediately swung open and he ran through.

This tunnel was very short and, before he could say "treasure", he was in a chamber filled with exactly that. He had never seen anything like it before. Piles and piles of every sort of valuable item you could think of. There were coins from all lands, swords, shields, crowns, jewellry, priceless gems, enormous chests (filled with even more treasure) and all sorts of other things. Coming back to reality, Rodger was collecting up everything he could see and stuffing it down his socks, in his pockets and even up his sleeves! When he had all he could carry he made his way to the other side of the chamber and crawled on his hands and knees through to a second, smaller chamber. Hurriedly, he jogged through these piles of treasure until he came to another tunnel. Cautiously, he popped his head through and found he was back on the other side of the hill. He had done it! He had got revenge! So the pixies never dared to go anywhere near Mower Hall ever again, whilst the goblins lived a happy, rich life.

Exploring For Hidden Treasure
by Harry Hawkins aged 8

Once there were two 14 year old boys called Zak and Jake who were the kind of boys that liked playing computer games. The boys were playing this computer game where you had to find hidden treasure, when suddenly they were sucked straight up inside the screen. "How did this happen?" squeaked Jake. They were very small.

"Ooh! Look, here's a letter," squeaked Zak.

This is what it read:

Dear Zak and Jake,

To escape you must find the treasure hidden in the game. But be very careful, there will be lots of terrible beasts along the way, such as the Wangdoodle, a big fierce monster that has long sharp canines. He will eat you if you're not careful. You will see the Wangdoodle if you go through the very left passage where the cave splits.

"Well this should be quite easy," said Jake, thinking about how good he is at computer games. But he was wrong. The screen took them to a large, dark and creepy cave in the middle of a desert.

"Com' on," said Jake.

"All right," whispered Zak, quite afraid by the expected appearance of things like the Wangdoodle the letter warned about.

So on they crept into a cave, exploring it until they

found somewhere that the cave split up.

"Oh no!" moaned Jake. "Another tragedy!"

"Should we go straight on?" asked Zak. "It hasn't been that bad yet has it?"

"No," said Jake. "That's a good idea actually."

"So what are we waiting for?" said Zak. "We want to get out of here, don't we Jake?"

"Yes we do," Jake agreed.

The two boys travelled on further into the cave when they saw a big signpost outside a den. The signpost said BEWARE OF THE DRAMPIRE. Zak and Jake suddenly felt scared and excited all at the same time. The boys had beaten the Drampire on the computer game before but it felt different in real life. Zak told Jake that he remembered how to get past the Drampire but they needed the golden axe. Jake noticed a brown and gold box near the entrance to the Drampire's den. "Look Zak," he shouted, "that might be the box from the computer game where you find the golden axe to slaughter the Drampire."

Zak and Jake crept quietly towards the den, trying not to disturb the Drampire. As they got near enough, the boys reached the box and started to open it. The box creaked loudly, just like Zak's Dad's garage door when it was opened. The Drampire heard the noise and got up slowly from his armchair (because he was tired after all the fighting on the computer games) and began walking towards the boys. Zak and Jake took their chance to lift the heavy golden axe from the box and were ready for action when the Drampire reached them. They lifted the axe over the Drampire's head.

"Go away you hideous beast," yelled Jake and Zak. "We're not scared of you."

When the Drampire saw the axe waving over his head and the two boys yelling at him he flew back into his den and hid under the covers of his bed. Zak and Jake chuckled a bit after that.

Suddenly another letter appeared in front of them. This time the letter did not look as old as the first one did. In fact it was gold with a medal on it.

The letter said:

CONGRATULATIONS

Zak and Jake, you have beaten the Drampire.

Now you have two more monsters to defeat (the Bulldramasse and the Oriosaurus). Some creatures will give you advice along the way.

GOOD LUCK

Next, they walked further through the cave. Soon they arrived at a tunnel that goes underground.

"Shall we go in there?" asked Zak, bravely.

"I don't know," whispered Jake, trembling a bit. "All right, let's go!" said Jake.

So they went into the tunnel and, about halfway through, they heard a noise – a scary noise. It seemed like a mixture of a giant roar and a creaky, rumbling sound. Then came big heavy footsteps.

"What could that be?" asked Jake, still trembling a little.

"Could it be the two monsters from the letter Zak?" whispered Jake.

"Here's our plan," said Zak. "We'll go out of the cave and crawl around on our hands and knees, then we can sneak up on the monsters, or whatever it is."

Jake and Zak got down and began crawling as sneakily as they could. Now they were both a bit frightened. Jake was still trembling and Zak had a funny kind of feeling that made him wobbly.

"Can I stay behind Jake?" Zak asked.

Jake told Zak he had to say with him. "I'm scared too."

Before long, the two boys saw something that looked as big as their bedroom at home. It looked like the shadow of a massive oak tree waving its branches in the dark. But this thing had spikes as big as swords at the top rather than little green leaves.

"Let's take a closer look, then we can see what it is," said Zak. He felt very brave. The boys carried on crawling up towards the thing. As they got closer, Zak noticed that there were two things.

"That's why we heard two sounds. It must be the two monsters from the letter."

The second monster was much smaller than the huge one. Jake realised that it must be the Bulldramasse and the Oriosaurus because he remembered them from playing the computer game. They both had armour made out of thick, strong iron. They both carried swords and the Oriosaurus also carried a dagger. In the computer game the monsters were Level 3, that meant Jake and Zak would have to try extra hard to defeat the monsters. They would be twice as difficult to defeat as the Drampire. Jake had only made it to Level 3 once or twice and was worried about their chances now.

The Oriosaurus was much smaller than the Bulldramasse. He was only two meters tall, which is small for a monster but not small for a kid who has to defeat it. The little monster was very good at running fast because he had a lot of practice running away from things he was scared of. The Oriosaurus was scared of things like shadows under his bed and all kinds of other monsters that come into the cave as well as all sorts of other things. He wouldn't be scared of two young, teenage boys though.

Before long the Oriosaurus saw the two boys crawling up to him sneakily. He told his friend, the Bulldramasse, about the boys.

"I'll deal with them," raged the Bulldramasse, who would do anything to protect his little friend.

Jake suddenly realised what was happening and yelled to Zak.

"You'll have to make a quick plan Zak, the big one is coming towards us."

Zak took a few minutes to think what to do, then he told Jake his plan.

"Here's what we'll do. You distract the Bulldramasse so that he can't see what's happening and I'll hide behind that tree and throw stones at the Oriosaurus. The Oriosaurus is bound to be scared and run away and the big Bulldramasse will follow. If we run fast enough the other way then we can get away from them, collect the treasure and go home.

So that's what they did and the plan was successful.

When Zak and Jake stopped running they could not see the monsters anymore, apart from two small, far away dots. When they got their breath back, they could see a beautiful, big glimmering box in front of them. The boys opened it and saw piles of gleaming, glittering treasure. On the floor, next to the treasure box, they saw a swirling, patterned circle drawn into the ground. This looked like the pattern on the computer screen when you were about to exit the game. The words "To the Blue Valley" were written in the centre of the circle. The Blue Valley was the name of the place where Zak and Jake lived. The boys were so excited and pleased to find they had beaten the game and were going home at last. The two boys stepped through the circle, carefully holding the beautiful box of treasure. The circle began to swirl round and round like magic and, before they knew it, Zak and Jake had landed on their drive.

They walked home happily with the treasure, which they kept hidden under the bed in their bedroom to help remember an amazing day.

Snowy Saturday
by Lucy Redfern aged 9

On a dark Christmas Eve it was snowing and all was fast asleep, dreaming of how their Christmas would turn out to be, except for one person – Father Christmas.

Father Christmas was putting all the presents in his sack when the clock struck twelve-o'clock. "Ho, ho, ho. I think I might get going now," and off he flew with the sack in the back of his sleigh. He travelled far and wide until he came to the last house. It was Mandy Silver's house. She wanted Santa to bring her a bike. One of those bikes... ha, yes, a racing bike, she wanted one of those. When Santa had delivered all the presents she wanted (well, almost all of them), he went back to his workshop where he said to all of his elves. "Now we are going to start building toys for next year. OK?"

"OK," the elves replied in little, squeaking voices.

When the morning came Mandy got up and went into her Mum and Dad's room and woke them up. "Can I open my stocking?" she asked excitedly.

"OK," said her Dad.

"Sure," said her Mum, yawning.

The first present she opened was some Funky Friends bubble bath and the second thing was ten candy canes in a box. When she had finished opening all the presents in her stocking, Mandy and her Mum and Dad went downstairs and opened the presents that were under the tree. Mandy thought she wasn't going to get a bike because it wasn't under the tree, but a few minutes passed and they went to the tree and got the cards from the branches that were sticking out. There was only one letter which was addressed to Mandy Silver. She opened it and it said:

Dear Mandy Silver

I have heard you have been a very good girl this year and I just want to say thank you for your Christmas list. Oh yes, I almost forgot to say, there is a surprise for you in the kitchen.

Have a nice Christmas and take care.

All our love. Father Christmas and the Elves.

"Wow," Mandy thought, a real letter from Father Christmas.

"It just goes to show how good you really can be," said her Mum.

So after, Mandy went into the kitchen and there was the bike she had always wanted. It was a....... RACING BIKE.

"Hurray," shouted Mandy excitedly.

So, when Mandy had got over her moments of daydreaming, her Dad said, "Mandy, what do you want for your breakfast?"

"Er, hot cross buns please Dad," replied Mandy.

"OK Mandy."

"Delicious," said Mandy, when she'd finished them.

"They're the best ones in the entire world!" said Mandy.

"Why thank you my dear," replied her Dad.

Back at the workshop, all of the elves were making the toys and things for next year. The elves were singing and the bells were ringing and all of them were down to work, even the Christmas dogs. The Christmas dogs had white fur with a bell around each of their necks with silver and gold string attached to the bell.

Back at home, where Mandy lived, there was a party going on. Lots and lots of people were there, even some of the neighbours' dogs and cats were there too.

A year had gone by and that Christmas night Father Christmas was putting the presents in the sleigh, but instead of Father Christmas going... THE DOGS DID!

A Touch Of Magic
by Rebecca Newington aged 9

Do you like looking at the stars? Well nine year old Lucy Willow-Wood thinks they are fascinating. One night, when Lucy was looking at the stars, she saw something very bright. Lucy had a feeling it was magic. There was a bright gold flash; it was a bit like lightning but much brighter. It was so bright Lucy closed her eyes, something strange happened next, but, as Lucy had her eyes closed, she couldn't see what happened. It felt like somebody was sprinkling some dust over her. Then she felt herself melt away into the sky. When she opened her eyes, she found herself flying through the sky. As she flew higher and higher and higher she began to see a figure. It looked a bit like a horse. As she got closer, she began to see it wasn't a horse, it was a unicorn! When Lucy reached the unicorn it began to speak.

"Hello Lucy, I'm Stardust," said the unicorn softly.

"H-h-how did you know my name?" stuttered Lucy.

"Because we've been trying to bring you back to our world," Stardust explained. "So, climb on my back and I'll take you there." Lucy quickly jumped onto Stardust's back and they both flew to Rainbow Dream. As they flew over Rainbow Dream, Lucy saw how beautiful it was. There was a beautiful, trickling stream which lead to a sparkling, multi-coloured waterfall in the middle of a huge, green forest. Next to the forest there was a sweet, little town where all the houses were pretty purple and white toadstools with cute, little windows. At the far side of the land there was a beautiful, shining castle made of shells which glistened in the bright sun. As they flew towards the castle, lots of little fairies came rushing out of their toadstool houses to greet them. As Stardust slowed down to land, a fairy King and Queen proudly strolled out of the castle's big, shiny yellow gates.

Stardust landed lightly on the bright green grass in front of the castle. Lucy hopped off Stardust's back onto the soft ground below.

"Hello Lucy. My name is Queen Sylvia," said the Queen

"And I am King Bronzo," said the King.

"Pleased to meet you," said Lucy, shyly.

"We need you to help us get rid of the evil Antonollyon...," the King managed to say, before he was rudely interrupted by a terrifying crash of thunder as the sky quickly turned a very dark black colour.

"What's happening?" yelled Lucy over the sound of the thunder.

"It's the evil Antonollyon, quick, we need to get into our houses!" cried one of the older fairies.

The King and Queen hurried inside, while Lucy was pushed through the huge gates by one of the castle guards. When they got inside they went straight to the basement for shelter. Once inside, the King explained that the evil Antonollyon had kidnapped his daughter, Princess Myera. She was being held hostage in his dark, dismal and damp den.

"How dreadful!" exclaimed Lucy.

"That's why we need you to help us," said the King.

"But why me?" asked Lucy.

"Because you look exactly like Princess Myera and you are the same age," said Queen Sylvia, "and you can trick the evil Antonollyon."

"Please can you help us get her back?" asked the King. "It's very important because it's her 10th birthday in a few days time and there is going to be a grand ball. We were going to give her her very first sparkling tiara and wand."

"I've heard there is a secret passage in this castle. We

must find it as it leads to the Antonollyon's den," replied one of the guards.

"So shall we start looking then?" asked Lucy.

"That sounds like a good idea," said the King. "I'll see if I can get some of the younger fairies to help you look."

Meanwhile..... the Antonollyon had locked the princess up in a cage which was hanging from the ceiling. He was teasing her by jeering and sniggering and calling her names.

Lucy looked high and low for the secret passage with some of the other fairies. After about half an hour, one of the fairies (called Anna) eventually found the secret passageway by pushing a stone with an inscription in Latin on it.

"What does it say on the stone?" Anna asked Lucy.

"I'm not sure, but I think it says whoever enters may never come out," Lucy replied.

"Well, we need to go in there and find the Princess, it's our only chance to get her back," replied another fairy called Jessie.

"Come on then, what are we waiting for?" said Lucy.

With that, Lucy, Anna and Jessie flew into the dark, slimy passage. Although they couldn't see anything to begin with, their eyes soon became used to the dark. The walls were damp and slimy.

"It's horrible in here," remarked Jessie.

"Yes, and I'm covered in slime," grumbled Lucy,

wiping a big bit of slime off her head.

Soon the passage became lighter and they could see a figure in the distance.

"I think that's Antonollyon," whispered Anna. "Who else would live in a dark, damp, dirty cave like this?"

"Good point," muttered Jessie.

"Come on, we haven't got time to waste. We need to sneak in there and rescue the Princess," said Lucy.

And with that, the three of them silently flew into the cave. They could see Antonollyon teasing the Princess, sniggering and sneering at her.

"Oh that must be terrible," remarked Jessie.

"Shhh!" went the other two.

As they sneaked around the side of the cave, they noticed the keys hanging right by a large, scary dog with sharp teeth.

"Come on, we need to get those keys and get the Princess out of here, I've got a plan. I'll go and distract Antonollyon. Anna, you distract the dog and Jessie, can you get the keys and free the Princess?" said Lucy.

"OK," agreed the other two.

So they set their plan to work. Lucy silently sneaked up behind Antonollyon then shouted, "Boo!" and made him jump out of his skin.

"Ha, ha," jeered Lucy, darting away as quick as she could before he had a chance to grab her leg. "Bet you can't catch me?"

"What, how, I don't understand?" How did you get

out?" Antonollyon said in a confused sort of way.

"I didn't," Lucy protested, as there was a fierce bark from the dog, Antonollyon swirled around to see Anna dodging the dog's sharp teeth. Behind his back, Jessie was quickly unlocking Myera's cage, and just in time too, because at that minute he swivelled round to see the Princess sneaking out of the cage.

"Get back here," he yelled.

"Quick," Lucy cried. "Get us out of here."

Just as they thought they were about to get caught, an idea popped into Anna's head. She got out her magic wand, said some magic words and, with a flash, all four of them were back in Myera's bedroom at the palace.

"Cool," thought Lucy. "I wish I could do that!"

At that moment, the King and Queen came rushing into the room to greet them. They were extremely pleased when they saw the four of them standing there, happily talking to each other. Lucy was invited to stay for a while so she could go to Myera's ball.

At the ball, Lucy, Anna and Jessie were each presented with a special golden pendant by the King and Queen. Lucy's had a beautiful crystal in the centre. Later on, the Queen explained to Lucy that if she wished to see Rainbow Dream, or even come back, she could do it by rubbing the crystal and saying some secret magic words.

After the ball, Lucy noticed that Stardust, the unicorn, had reappeared and knew it was time to go home. She said goodbye to everybody and jumped onto the Unicorn's back. As Stardust lifted up into the sky, Lucy called goodbye and waved to everyone in Rainbow Dream as they all waved back to her. When Stardust arrived at the point where she had met Lucy, Lucy climbed off her back and gave the unicorn a big hug and wished her goodbye. As she began to wonder what was going to happen next, a strange tingling feeling came over her. She must have fallen asleep because when she woke up her mum was calling her. Had it all been a dream, she asked herself. She looked down and saw the necklace. It couldn't have been a dream. She looked into the crystal on the necklace to see a face smiling back at her. That's an adventure I'll never forget, Lucy thought to herself as she went down for tea.

The School Bully
by Gabrielle Amelia McGregor aged 8

James was the school bully. Dunston Secondary School was his bullying grounds, there were a group of kids James always bullied. So the kids decided to come up with a plan to get their own back on James.

James was large for his age, never changed his clothes, never had a wash and never combed his hair. So the kids thought what can't he do. Then the kids came up with the perfect plan. The Spring Fair was coming up so the kids volunteered him on the sponge throwing stall, then they told him. When the big day came they couldn't stop laughing. So he got off the stall and said, "I will never bully you again, but don't put me back on that stall." So the kids said, "OK," and James became best friends with the kids.

What Shall I Get For My Mum
by Teah Degnen-Brown aged 9

Hi, my name's called Nickolus and I'm having some trouble what to get for my mum. You see, it's Mothers Day soon and I haven't got my mum anything.

"Nickolus, tea's ready." That's my little sister, she thinks she's my mum.

"NICKOLUS"

"OK, I'm coming."

"Nickolus, what shall we get for Mum?" That's my dad, he's in the army.

"I know, I know – a candle."

"What are you fighting over now?"

Naughty us! "We were just playing Mum."

"Nickolus," Dad said in a whispering voice. "We will find a present for your mum tomorrow. OK?"

It's now morning. "Dad, you promised that we would go and get a present for Mum."

"OK. Hellan, are you coming?"

"Yes Dad."

So we went to the shops. What about a mat? No a cat. No a hat. What about a new car? Great idea! Where are we going to get the money from? Maybe we could do jobs. "Let's do it then."

So we done it, it took us two days.

"One more house Dad, but do we have to do Mrs Doomse's house?"

"It's the only thing to get Mum a car."

"But Dad, she might eat us."

"Let's knock then."

"I don't know why you're scared of Mrs Doomse. I like her, she's spooky. Oh – hello Mrs Doomse, we're doing ch-ch-chores around people's houses and we were wondering if we could do yours. I-i-if that's OK with you?"

"Yes, come in," she sounded like a witch. In fact, she is a witch.

"Now, the living room needs doing." It looked like a farm and smelt like fish.

"Well, I'm glad that's done. Oh no! The money! Come back money. We've only got a dollar. Let's go and get her a box of chocolates."

"Yes, OK then."

"Dad, Dad. Wake up. It's Mothers Day. Let's get the chocolates and I'll get Mum.

"HAPPY VALENTINE'S DAY!"

"Oh why thank you, but I don't care if you only got me a box of chocolates, all I want is you three."

Trapped In The Snow
by Rebecca Taylor aged 10

One snowy, windy day, three people called Lindy, Simon and Alice went for a very long walk that was meant to be taken by car, but they needed a lot of exercise. On the way, Alice fell down a hole, it was as deep as the long, wavey sea. She couldn't get out. Her mother, Lindy, didn't see her fall down the hole and neither did her friend, Simon. When Lindy and Simon had noticed she wasn't there, they began to shout. "Alice. Oh Alice," but she didn't answer so they kept shouting her. The third time they shouted her she was shouting back, "I'm down here. Follow my voice."

"OK," Simon replied. So they followed her voice. When they did get to her she said, "I've found something like a passage."

"What does it look like?" said her mum.

"It's just a dark tunnel really."

"Oh, OK," replied her mum.

"Can you two jump down here so we can crawl through it?"

"Erm?"

"OK," said Lindy.

When they both jumped down it was as loud as a fire-drill. It was also as smokey as a fire.

"Where is the tunnel?" asked Simon excitedly.

She pointed out where it was, "Over there."

"OK," he said back.

"Come on then, if we're going," said Lindy.

"OK Mum," said Alice.

Simon went first because he knew where he was going. When they got half way through they came to a point where there was three tunnels. There was a right tunnel, a left tunnel and a forward tunnel. They chose to go left because Simon always felt lucky going left. The tunnel was very dark, but as they were getting further down the tunnel they saw light.

"It's a miracle," laughed Simon.

"Ha ha, yeah," laughed Alice.

"It's getting lighter," shouted Simon and Alice.

"OK kids, here we are. Let me get to the front to boost you two up," said Lindy, because she was at the back.

"Right then, come on Simon," said Lindy.

"OK," said Simon.

"You are quite heavy aren't you?" laughed Lindy.

"Yeah," said Simon.

"Hurry up," said Alice.

"Alright, alright. I'm up."

"OK then Alice, your turn."

"Right, coming," said Alice.

"You're much lighter," said Lindy, picking her up.

"There, now you're out it's my turn."

"There's a car, it can help us get back," shouted Alice.

"OK," said Lindy and Simon.

"I'm driving," said Lindy. "I do have a licence you know!"

"I'm in the front," shouted Alice.

"OK," said Simon.

So they all got in the car and went home. And, when they got home, they told all their family and friends the whole story.

The Dragon's Cave
by Chantal Ratcliffe aged 9

As I trembled through the overgrown grass, I looked straight into the centre of a dark, gloomy cave, my heart thumped like a giant's foot banging on the ground. The stream that ran down the triangular cliffside was as clear as crystals. The brown, freaky tree that stood outside the cave, as if it was a guard, had long bent arms that drooped over me, it had red, evil eyes that constantly stared. My mind suddenly switched from the frightening surroundings to something calling.

I don't know who, what or why. I swung my head round, there was nothing there, and the long, narrow, horribly steep path was no longer there. It had gone, basically disappeared! Now my only true hope was that the dark, gloomy cave was my way home.

I took a giant step inside, I felt I was in danger. I took my time taking step by step in a slow pace. I could hear the howling of the wind and I could feel it gently blowing through my hair and on my ears. Really, I wanted to get out of here, but all around me was black so, bravely, I carried on taking step by step in my usual slow pace. I remembered my pack-bag; it had food which I did and didn't like. I took my lemonade out and had a sip, suddenly my lemonade began to glow, I was amazed. I stood up and made my way once again along the cave.

It was like there was no ending to this cave, but I travelled on..... suddenly, the dark surroundings changed into an amazing place. Short, green grass and a small, beige path lead up to a long bridge that was dark brown and polished, the water underneath the bridge was clearer than crystals! And, in the distance, I could just make out a boat in the shape of a dragon. I sat down on a long, blue bench. I waited quietly until someone called my name. "Liz." I looked around thinking it was my dad but then I saw a man nothing like my dad. What surprised me greatly was that he knew my name. Then I remembered my jumper, it had LIZ written on the back.

"Now," he said, "I am on a journey to kill a dragon. I need anyone to help me."

"I am willing to help sir!" I exclaimed excitedly.

We didn't talk for the rest of the journey. I was too frightened to talk anyway, I just thought of what might happen to me, like having my head bitten off or being eaten whole by a dragon! Finally we got there. Before we got off the boat, the man gave me a long narrow sword and a shotgun. We both tramped through the tall grass, careful not to wake the curled up dragon that lay at the mouth of the cave. The dragon had a diamond shaped symbol on its forehead. I trembled as I passed the dragon, then I heard a sound and the smell of smoke circled in my nose.

I looked around, the man had gone and in his place was a pile of thick, red blood. I screamed ... then turned ... the dragon was lying down in an eternal sleep and the symbol on its forehead was fading. The dragon was dead! My heart lit up like a firework. But I didn't kill it, the man that was sent didn't kill him, for he was in the dragon's body, wasn't he?

The Letter
by Ashleigh Whitehead aged 11

It was a dark, misty morning, the wind was howling.

"Oh, I don't want to go to work," groaned Andrew.

"You have to, we'll get more money for the house, besides I need you out of the house so I can get the new furniture in," nagged Lisa.

"Oh all right, anything to make you happy."

Lisa smiled as she made the bed.

"See you later," shouted Andrew up the stairs.

"Bye!"

Andrew went to work for the day.

Lisa made herself a small breakfast and finished arranging the furniture. On the settee, there in front of her, she suddenly saw the collar of Shadow (her dead cat).

Knock! Knock!

Lisa went to open the door and asked the stranger who he was.

"Ethan," he replied.

Ethan was a small, scruffy boy. He had red marks all over him and he was crying. Ethan was from the mill. "I got beaten again," he whimpered. "Sir beat me for talking."

"Oh well, why don't you come in and sit down?"

"Thanks."

Lisa got Ethan a cup of water and a slice of bread.

Knock! Knock!

Lisa again went to open the door, it was Andrew.

"Hi honey."

"What's going on?" Andrew asked.

"This here is Ethan, he is from the mill, he has no house and no food or water," explained Lisa.

"Why don't you stay with us for a while, you can stay in the spare room if you like?"

Andrew went out and got changed then showed Ethan to his room. After a while, Lisa came upstairs to the bedroom. "What are you doing, you've been ages up here?"

"Me and Ethan were just talking about Shadow, our cat. Ethan said he had a cat called Shadow as well and he described it, the same as ours."

"Can I please see your cat?" Ethan asked.

"I'm sorry dear, but Shadow is dead now," Lisa

explained. "He used to stay in this room."

Lisa, Andrew and Ethan all went downstairs to have some tea. It got late and everyone decided to go to bed.

"Andrew, wake up! I'm going checking on Ethan."

When Lisa went into the spare room Ethan ran up to her and said he could hear a meowing noise and could see a shadow of a cat.

"There is no cat in here but there should be a few outside."

The next morning everybody got up and dressed.

"Where are you going?" Ethan asked.

"To the orphanage," Andrew replied.

When they got to the orphanage a lady said that he could come in a week. Andrew and Lisa told Ethan the news. He seemed okay with everything, but that night was different to what they had in mind. Ethan rushed into their bedroom and shouted for them to get up because there was a fire downstairs. Andrew and Lisa called somebody to look in the house and see what could have caused it. Andrew grabbed a couple of buckets of water to put the fire out.

"Well, all I can see here is a cat's claw which has cut the wire," the Fire Inspector said.

"How? We don't have a cat."

"We used to have Shadow, but she's dead."

"Shadow is alive, she comes in my room," said Ethan.

"No she can't, she is dead. It must be another cat."

Ethan took Andrew and Lisa up to the spare room and

there, on the bed, lay Shadow.

"It's a ghost of Shadow," commented Andrew.

"Bye."

Lisa went downstairs to say bye to the Fire Inspector.

"Thank you for helping."

The door slammed as loudly as a lion's roar.

"I think we should get to the orphanage." Lisa and Andrew took him to the orphanage. "See you soon."

Ethan waved then turned around and disappeared.

"Whoa, where did Ethan just go?"

"I don't know Andrew!" Lisa replied.

"Maybe he's a ghost, like Shadow!"

That night Lisa went up to the spare room to clean up, but when she got there there was a letter on the pillow. It read:-

Dear Andrew and Lisa

You probably want to know why I first came to you. Well, I can't tell you right now but I will be back. Until then, whatever you do, do not go into the spare room."

Love from Ethan

Tramp

by Daisy Whewell aged 10

I slowly sat down, I felt weaker and weaker, I didn't think I could move. My dark hair felt like straw, my face felt cold, my legs started to tremble and my hands were already shaking. My ragged clothes blew about in the wind.

I tried to cuddle up to some dustbins in a dark ally, but they were stiff and made me feel even colder. I stood back up and looked around for a nicer place to sleep. Suddenly, I heard a noise, a crashing noise, it was close and I started running back down the ally. What could it be? My heart was beating faster and faster. I heard the padding of footsteps coming closer and closer. I slowly turned around and took a deep breath. I saw a dark shape moving towards me. Phew! It was just a cat, my heart slowed down 'till it was at its normal rate, that was the only normal thing since my mum and dad both died from cancer.

I knelt down to pet the cat, it was soft and black. I saw it was limping so I looked at his legs and I felt up and down three of his legs. I would not touch the fourth leg because it was bent the opposite way to the other legs. I cuddled up to the cat to keep warm but the cat hissed and limped off into the darkness and then I was alone again. I climbed into the dustbin and settled down to sleep.

I woke up and it was all dark, I started to panic. I yelled and screamed, I couldn't get the lid off. I heard footsteps outside, a boy opened the lid, I could see light. "Thank you, thank you," I said to the boy. He was tall, he had brown hair, he was perfect in every way, but I was so embarrassed I was in a dustbin. "Hi," I said. He just stared at me. I asked him what he was looking at.

"You," he said in a floaty voice.

"Why?" I said, getting more and more puzzled.

133

"Because you're so sad," he answered, still in his floaty voice. Then he lifted me out of the dustbin. I felt so happy now and I wanted to stay with this boy forever.

I found out that he wasn't a boy, he was a man working for social services and was trying to get me a new home. I told him that I didn't want a new home, but he wouldn't listen.

I am now happy he didn't listen to me because I am living in a lovely home with loving parents, they are not my own but I still love them.

The Trip That Never Was
by James Southworth aged 10

One bright sunny Wednesday afternoon, two best friends, Tim and Tom, were desperate to get out of school. If you would like to find out why just keep on reading, but it is extremely unpleasant. OK, back to the story.

Tom was stretching out his long arms, staring at the clock, but to his misfortune it had stopped. He stared at his watch, but that had stopped too. It seemed that everyone was looking at their watches and there was an echo going round the class saying, my watch has stopped. Weird!

Tim, on the other hand, was pointing his short chubby fingers at the old mansion on the edge of the cliff, looking out to sea. To everyone's luck the bell rang and Tim and Tom had an idea. Why had they not thought of it before? They were going to go to the old mansion and explore it.

Tim rang his mum to tell her he and Tom would be home late.

Off they trudged up the long windy road to the old mansion. Suddenly there was a huge BANG and a window smashed. Then, to make it worse, there was a lady screaming. As they approached the old mouldy, wooden doors of the mansion, a beam of light came out and ripped out their souls. Were they alive... or dead? Alive, but only just.

BANG! There was that noise again, and the same scream. SMACK! The doors had shut tight. Both the boys agreed that they had to find a new way out. But how? As Tom looked at the stained glass windows he noticed that it was just like his new game on his Xbox, Doom 3. He told Tim and he agreed. They battled on and fought beasts like the triple-eyed aliens, the five-horned bull and, last of all, the Pyder, a 50 ft monster, half python and half spider.

Tom looked at his watch, still broke. They walked down the hallway and there it was. It was more deadly than the Pyder, it was the DEVIL. Tom noticed a keypad on his left arm. He pushed a button and, as if by magic, he had a bow and arrow. Tim did exactly the same. They fired fast and furious. Tim told Tom he was going to die, so he pushed a button and he vanished.

It was all up to Tom, but the force of the DEVIL was too strong. Tom pressed buttons frantically, but he couldn't seem to vanish. But, all of a sudden, he pressed the "Do Not Touch" button and he vanished!

It was black and slowly they began to see things again. They realised that they were in Tim's room playing on Doom 3 in the exact same point as they were a few minutes ago. So, when you play video games, maybe it's for real!!!

A Ghostly Friend
by George Johnson aged 10

"You're not going out messing around the old paper mill again are you Robbie?" his dad said. Robbie shrugged and hunched his shoulders up and down like a clockwork toy. He knew he really was, but he slouched and climbed the stairs until his parents fell asleep.

As Robbie closed the door behind him, he felt a mysterious feeling that sent a shiver up his spine. He ran through the rain that beat down like a coppersmith's hammer. He jogged towards the mill that gave him an eerie feeling. After becoming bored messing about in the rubble, he sprinted into the mill. As he walked in, the door groaned as it shut behind him. Startled, he jumped backwards, falling into a hole. He tumbled down, hitting the sides until he regained a grip on the sides. As he looked down, he saw a pearl-white figure with its back to him. The figure turned and looked directly at him. Paralysed with fear, Robbie remained completely tranquil. As the figure glided towards him, Robbie saw that his feet didn't touch the floor. As it looked up, Robbie saw that its face was paralysed with fear, just like Robbie's.

"Who are you?" Robbie said, feeling a bit braver.

"Samuel Stamford," it replied, holding out a hand.

Robbie took it and, as he shook it, he felt as though his hand had been plunged into ice cold water.

"What are you doing here?" Robbie asked.

"I work here for the overseer because he's still in charge. As we died here we have to haunt this place," he replied.

"But why won't he let you go?" Robbie said.

"It's because I keep asking, but he only says no," he replied.

"Where is his office?" Robbie asked.

After a discussion, the overseer let Samuel go.

"How can I repay you?" Samuel asked.

"You can make sure nobody knows I was here," Robbie said.

Instantly, the overseer stepped forward and clicked his fingers. Robbie saw black, then, after a while, he fell asleep.

When Robbie woke, he realised he was being carried by a tall figure. Robbie's brain was trying to make out the noise. He saw that there was a machine that he had seen smashed. He asked the man, "What year is it?"

"1890," the man answered.

Robbie panicked, trapped!

As far as we know, Robbie's ghost is roaming the earth in search of the overseer.

The Ghost

by Reece Derrett aged 10

Thud! The blind shot up. I turned around to see a shadow in the dark, dismal sky. I crept over to the threadbare blind to close it, as I did I heard a tremendous crash – what was it?

The next day I was walking to school, when I arrived I sat down. Suddenly, I felt a chill up my spine. I shivered and put my jumper on. When I turned around all of my stuff was gone. I asked my friend if he had seen it but he hadn't.

I was walking home from school and suddenly I tripped over, but there was nothing there. I soon realised I had football practise and I only had half an hour. I ran home and got my kit but couldn't find my football. It had vanished! What am I going to do, I thought. I looked at my watch, I had 5 minutes. It was too late, I'd missed the start of training. I dropped my stuff and walked over to my bedroom door. I was about to walk out when it slammed shut. I fell back and hit my head on the table. I was scared. I got up and tried it again. When I finally got out it was time for tea, so I went into the kitchen. As I was eating, my plate fell off the table. Suddenly, I heard an ear-splitting crash! I got up from the table and dawdled up to my room. I sat on my bed thinking what could be causing all these strange happenings – could it be a ghost? No, of course not... or could it? I was too caught up in the mystery to notice my TV had been turned on. All of a sudden the TV flashed on and said that 14 children were killed in a coach accident. I know all of them, they go to the same football practise as me. Could the ghost have saved my life by taking my football?

A Story
by James Collins aged 11

It was a dark, windy night and Captain Bobs and his patrol squad were scouting out the area, but so far they had found nothing. Slowly and cautiously they moved through the silent landscape, guns ready to shoot the first thing that moved, when suddenly there was a rustle behind them. Raising their guns they span around ready to fire.

"Stop," commanded Captain Bobs. There was another rustle, then a gunshot and Captain Bobs staggered forward, hands outstretched, then collapsed dead.

Suddenly, lots of tiny men stepped out and with their golden swords, they made short work of the squad. Nearby, another Scout Squad had heard the screams of pain from the one which was under attack and quickly got to the place where they were.

"Jumping Jacklegs, it's the Guardians," yelled the Captain of the investigating squad. "Well, don't just stand there – FIRE!"

There was a horrible sound as the thousands of bullets buried themselves in the monsters' hearts.

"Fall back, fall back. We'll deal with the Guardians," yelled the Captain to the survivors of the last squad.

"Sir, there is more coming, we need to....," the soldier stopped talking and looked at his chest. There was a golden blade sticking out of it, he tried to speak but blood came out of his mouth, then he crumpled to the ground.

"Get the hell out of here and that's an order, we can't win this battle," the Captain commanded. As he turned to run, a massive creature blocked his way. "Av... Av... Av...," he stammered.

"Avatar," the creature told him and, with one swift manoeuvre of his sword, he chopped the Captain's head off and ran to slaughter the rest of his men.

An Ordinary Night
by Jenny Castle aged 15

It was an ordinary night, or ordinary to Laura anyway, though it may not be to you – I don't know – for everybody has a different ordinary. The sky was a marbled grey, ebbing into navy around its rims, and the green leaves hung drowsily, weighted with droplets from previous rainfall.

Laura continued to stare lazily into space, as so many of us do from time to time. Lost in an alcove of thoughts, far from the chair in which she sat, by the window of her room, on the second floor of her home, at the edge of the village.

Sitting so still, as it were, so indifferent to the world around her, she failed to notice the boy. The small, shadow-like boy, as he passed between the hedgerows and through the garden gate; where he disappeared behind the rotting wood and dusty glass of the old shed door...

Sunlight filtered through the curtains of Laura's room, falling lightly onto the pillow of her bed and illuminating her sleeping face. Her dark eyes hidden, guarded by neat rows of short, curly brown lashes, and her lightly tanned cheeks flushed with warmth. Her pale pink lips parted a little, muttering softly, as the sounds of chattering birds and the scent of burning toast drew her slowly into consciousness.

"Laur-aaa!" A small, sandy coloured head poked itself around the corner of Laura's bedroom door, "Mum says it's time to get up."

"Mmmm," Laura rolled over and pulled the covers up to her head.

"You have to get up. Mum says so, Grandma's coming today."

Grumbling, Laura began to drag herself out of her bed and made her way towards the bathroom. Grandma was coming. More than anything else, this meant that the whole house would have to undergo a major cleaning frenzy. The floors would have to be vacuumed, the mantlepiece would have to be polished and, by the time her mother finished, every pot on the shelf would sparkle. This was not a prospect that filled Laura with joy – she knew that when she went down there was bound to be a job there, just waiting for her.

"Laura! Are you up yet?" Her mother's voice came drifting up the stairs, "Hurry up and get dressed! I want you to come and help me tidy up for when your Grandmother gets here. You can start by raking up those leaves – they get everywhere, and they're starting to rot…"

Half an hour later, Laura was up, dressed and stood at the back door, ready and poised, surveying the scene before her. The fallen leaves from surrounding trees had all blown across into their garden and scattered themselves over the lawn. Earlier on in the month they had looked pretty and bright, with their wild, autumn colours of red and gold. Now they were rotting. They had lost their crispness and their beautiful, October hues had been replaced by a slug-like brown. She crammed her feet into her wellies and began to slouch across the grass towards the shed.

Humming softly to herself Laura approached the shed, leaving behind her a trail of footprints in the fresh-laid dew. Taking hold of the latch she pushed back the old shed door, it creaked a little on its rusty hinges then swung open in a cloud of dust.

Laura stepped inside, blinking in the gloom, a shaft of sunlight filtered through the open door illuminating a small pile of grubby cloth heaped against the wall. It just so happened that Laura's attention was drawn to this one point and it also happened that, just as Laura looked, the pile of cloth started to stir. Laura let out a scream.

At the sound of Laura's high-pitched scream, the pile of cloth leapt up, looked about itself in confusion and proceeded to join in with Laura's screaming. Thereafter ensued a time of great confusion in which both girl and pile of cloth began to run blindly about the shed, setting tools and pots and paints in turmoil. Then, all at once, the two stopped screaming for, as the grips of their terror eased, the pile of cloth began to realise that Laura was only a girl and Laura began to realise that the pile of cloth was not a pile of cloth after all, but a boy.

The two stood in silence, each staring at the other. After a moment, Laura began to pluck up the courage to speak but, just as she opened her mouth, the words died on her tongue. In the midst of the kafuffle, neither of the pair had noticed the appearance of another but, as Laura gaped, from amongst the shadows emerged a creature, lightly padding its way towards the boy. Laura looked on in awe. It was a small creature, no bigger than a common cat, but with a tail nearly twice its size, giving the whole animal a rather unbalanced look – as if at any moment it may topple backwards from the position it currently took upon the shoulders of the boy.

Its nose was long and pointed with whiskers protruding from its damp and pinkish tip, its wide ears quivered on its head and its eyes, slanted and round, the colour of coals as they burn in the grate – flecked with the light of a street lamp as it begins to warm up, gazed at her questioningly. But its coat was what made Laura stare - silvery-grey, blue as the mist, as if the sky itself was reflected in its fur and the moonlight shone from its skin. "Voradae," said the boy, "he's called Voradae."

The sound of his voice brought Laura back to earth and she saw again the strangeness of the situation. Tearing her gaze from the creature she began to study the boy.

He looked to be about her age but skinnier, very much skinnier, and paler too. He stared at her hard from beneath his thick, black lashes, almost as if he were afraid she might strike out at any moment. His hair was as black as the night making his pasty complexion seem all the whiter and, as he stood there before her, her attention was drawn to his ears. To begin with they seemed normal enough – even if slightly longer than the average person – but as she studied them harder she noticed that the tops, unlike yours or mine, were pointed where they should be rounded.

"What are you?" she asked.

"I'm an elf," he replied, "and I need to ask your help."

Now you are probably already quite familiar with elves, after all they are found in so many fairy tales and between the covers of numerous books. But, as you may have noticed, there are differences for, just as no two humans are the same, no two elves are the same, and just as we humans have our nationalities, elves have their colonies. This particular elf, at which Laura was currently gawping in a most unladylike fashion, was an Everbeam elf. Everbeam elves are one of the very few remaining British colonies and their numbers are fast declining. You see, we humans have been so wrapped up in our own lives that we no longer take into account the life of any other species that happens to get in the way and, as a result, we have pushed the elves out of their homes and so far away that people have even come to question their existence.

Those who managed to survive have either been driven into the hills and mountains and down into the forests or, as many of them chose to do, stayed where they were and simply married into mortal homes. It may even be that, if you are very lucky, you have one living right next door to you now. If, at all, you suspect this then next time you see them just take an extra close look at their ears. Check for that extra little pointyness, you never know.

But, you see, for elves, finding a new home was not the end of their problems; elves are magical creatures and, as with any magical creature, they have to be extra careful with how they use their magic. It cannot last forever, it must be topped up and it can only be topped up from certain points. This, for the elves, is where their second problem begins. It is the only time when an elf must risk getting back to the place where their family was born.

At last, Laura could stand the silence no more, "Why are you here?" she asked.

"I'm lost," he said quite calmly, Laura thought, for a small boy who appeared to be completely alone except for his pet. "I was trying to get to Fells Peak to top up my powers when a farmer saw me and set his dogs on me, I ran and I hid, I came here to sleep because I thought it looked safe. It reminded me of a place in the stories my grandfather used to tell me about my great aunt and her mortal husband... I'm sorry I scared you, will you help me... please?"

"Of course I'll help you," Laura answered, recovering from disbelief, "but why Fells Peak? How can you 'top up your powers'?"

"I have to go there," he said, "because it was my Grandfather's h-."

But he never finished his sentence because, just at that moment, a car pulled up in the drive and a door slammed and the sound of footsteps could be heard clipping their way round to the side of the house. Both the elf and girl froze.

"Laura? Is that you? I thought I heard voices round the back," the shed door creaked open once more, "I-."

Her Grandmother stopped mid sentence, she looked at the elf, shook her head and looked again, then said, "I just wanted to say hello before I went in, is your mother in the house?"

"Y-yes, but-."

"But nothing. I'll see you in the house, you'd better wash those hands when you come in – it's filthy in here." And with that, her Grandmother left the shed and headed for the kitchen door.

Laura paused for a moment, unsure what to think, then turned back to the elf.

"What's your name?" she asked.

"Sasha," he replied.

"So what have you been up to since I saw you last? It feels so strange coming here to visit you, it used to be the other way round! You've certainly made it your own though." Grandma leaned forward expectantly, knife and fork poised over her plate. Laura looked down at her food, she couldn't concentrate, she continued to line up her peas around the edge of her plate, swinging her legs beneath her chair. She itched to get outside again, into the shed.

There was so much to do. She had said she would help Sasha, she had said she could get him to Fells Peak, it wasn't far away, once he was there he would be fine – he would have his magic again - but Laura had to get him there. That wouldn't be so easy, especially as they couldn't go by road.

"Can I get down now please Mum?"

"I suppose so, but I don't see what the rush is, you haven't even had dessert." Mum looked at her disapprovingly.

"Oh, there's always a rush nowadays," said Gran, "but all the same, you need to eat, take your pud with you. You're going to need some food in you."

Gratefully, Laura took the sticky bun which her grandmother held out for her, not stopping to think about what she had meant, and made her way upstairs to pack her bag ready for her mission.

Click. Laura heard the last of the lights being turned off. She waited ten more minutes and then began to climb out of her bed. Tiptoeing across her room, Laura pulled on her jacket and picked up her bag. Hardly daring to breathe, she made her way downstairs and out of the back door.

It was dark outside and the air was moist, filled with the scents of wet grass and burning wood.

"Are you there?" she whispered.

"Yes." came the reply from somewhere beside her.

She felt the goosebumps rise on her skin as the soft fur of Voradae brushed against her leg.

"Ready?" she said.

"Ready," said Sasha.

An hour later and the two were making their way over the moonlit fields, Voradae skipping ahead of them and doubling back every so often. Laura watched him. It took her mind off the millions of thoughts which flew round her head.

"Nearly there," she panted. They had been walking fast, but as they neared their destination Laura slowed – it was almost as if she didn't want to arrive. She didn't want to lose her new friend, she had only known him a day and already it felt like a lifetime. There was so much she wanted to ask and to learn but, all too soon, they arrived at Fells Peak.

"This is it," Laura's voice shook as she spoke, "this is Fells Peak."

Sasha nodded and stepped forward, slowly he began to speak – turning all the while,

"Valleys and peaks,

Wild moors, marshes bleak,

I call to the fairies,

I ask you to speak."

As he spoke Laura watched and, as Laura watched, the ground beneath her began to spin and the stars became a spiral and she felt her feet come away from the grass. She was floating.

"Great hurling seas,

Forests of trees,

I call to the fairies,

Restore power to me!"

And the world spun faster and the sky became closer and the stars began to fall to her feet. Then it stopped. Laura wobbled for a moment then lifted her head and looked about her. The air around was filled with lights. Small, dancing lights, like stars on a yo-yo string they bounced about before her eyes.

"Fairies!" she whispered. And she was right. The air was filled with fairies.

Now, I'd like to take this moment to set a nasty rumour

to rest. Not all fairies are spiteful and stubborn. It is just unfortunate that one of the most famous fairies of all, Tinkerbell, was. It seems such a shame that Tinkerbell gave fairies such a bad reputation, that it really ought to be put right as to what they are really like. Fairies are soft and gentle creatures, mystical and rarely seen due to an incredible shyness. It is these beautiful, winged people who keep the rest of the magical population supplied with their powers, they are, after all, the only ones who can be trusted to always be fair and honest.

Laura gazed in wonder as one by one the fairies swooped down and ever so gently kissed the top of Sasha's head. As the last one fluttered away he looked up at Laura and smiled.

"Thank you," he said, "I can make my own way now, but I'll make sure you get home safely without being seen by your mother. Just close your eyes and the fairies will take you back. Thank you again and remember, if you are ever in need of anything, all you have to do is wish."

And with that, Laura closed her eyes and felt the weight of her body fall away and her thoughts begin to wander…

Sunlight filtered through the curtains of Laura's room, falling lightly onto the pillow of her bed and illuminating her sleeping face. Her dark eyes hidden, guarded by neat rows of short, curly brown lashes and her lightly tanned cheeks flushed with warmth. Her pale pink lips parted a little, muttering softly, as the sounds of chattering birds and the scent of burning toast drew her slowly into consciousness.

"Laur-aaa!" A small, sandy coloured head poked itself around the corner of Laura's bedroom door, "Mum says it's time to get up."

"Mmmm," Laura rolled over and pulled the covers up to her head. What an amazing dream, no, not a dream. She pulled the covers back, she was still in her clothes and clinging to the leg of her trousers was an unmistakable hair. The hair of a creature that was not from this world. Slowly it all began to fall into place.

"Laura! Are you awake? I brought you some breakfast," came her grandmother's voice from the other side of the door.

Laura scrambled to pull the covers back up over her clothes. The bedroom door opened.

"Morning, did you have a good night?"

Did she have a good night? What a strange thing to say, unless… How much did her grandmother know? Gran passed her the plate and stood up tucking her tightly permed hair behind her ear. Laura watched her. Was it her or were her Grandmother's ears just that little bit pointier than the average persons…

The Robber's Tale
by Kirsty Haken aged 15

Darkness. Decay. The silent scene stank of them, gravestones reaching up to the air like their owners' hands stretching up, trying to escape. Cold, wet grass making the intruder slip and stumble through the icy night, the candle he held flickering as if threatening to go out.

A tall, sinister building rose up into this dark night, a house of death lying open for its next victim to come wandering freely into its wide-open jaws. This is where the intruder hastened to, regaining his composure as he made it to the stone walls of the tomb. Then, breathing his final breath of fresh air as he entered the crypt, he didn't know that his fate was upon him.

"I'm not afraid, I'm not! I'm not afraid." The constant mumble of the grave robber's voice was the only sound that filled the ancient chamber apart from the crackling of the candle, sharp like a whip.

In the middle of the room stood a stone box, a large oblong sarcophagus. On one side of the room stood a row of candlesticks, cobwebs laced between them and dust on their once golden stands. To the other side, on a stone shelf, stood more gold, this time they were cups and plates embellished with crests and covered, again, with dust and cobwebs, all except one.

This cup was the brightest of all, gleaming as if polished. What a prize! The robber could not resist it. Gently, he placed the candle down on the shelf and, slowly, clasped his hands around this trophy and lifted it towards him, raising it as if he would drink from it. Then he lowered it and examined it, inside was a ring, but a ring like never seen before, encrusted with sapphires, diamonds, rubies, amethysts, emeralds, encased in gold so pure it reflected every ray of light from the wandering candle flame. This was no trinket!

He couldn't resist, he held out his finger and placed the ring onto it, slipping it down onto his quivering finger and examining his hand. Perfect! He smiled, then frowned and then he gave a gasp of pain, which soon turned into a scream of agony.

As the ring glowed white hot, another scream echoed around the cavernous room. A new scream. A different voice. In the middle of the tomb, a stone coffin stood engraved with symbols of some strange language like the encryption of some ancient spell. This was where this new scream sounded from, one long, high pitched note which changed and formed a cackling laughter in the space of seconds, a strong malice held in its tone.

The intruder's eyes widened with terror and he stumbled backwards, arms flailing, the ring still a burning ring of fire against his finger, emitting strong white beams of blinding light which spread out to encase their victim with the scalding heat of a fire's centre.

In the middle of the room, the coffin too was glowing with the same unworldly light, shaking, trembling until the lid separated itself from the rest of it and fell with an echoing thud onto the hard concrete floor. The robber then beheld the horror that dwelled within its chest.

It was human shaped with a head, legs, arms and a torso, but all these features were distorted, the head was only half covered in flesh, the rest hung off its cheeks, forehead, chin and nose, rotting and blooded. Its eyes were slits without eyelids, the entire ball of each eye was cloudy white even the pupils, with blue blood vessels cutting through them. Its mouth was stripped of the lips leaving drooping skin, ragged and uneven with veins and nerve endings, dangling from the tattered remains of its lower face.

Its arms were sliced, with dried blood caked around the open wounds. The fingers were gnarled and skinless, clenched in mighty fists. There were holes in the wrists where occasionally the fat, lazy maggots crawled in and out of their host, using hundreds of tunnels they had burrowed into the corpse.

Its legs were turned outwards and the angle they were at suggested that they were disconnected from the joints and whenever it tried to walk they would crack and splinter. The bones in both legs stuck out of the muscle and the remaining skin giving the body the guise of a cripple.

The torso; the torso was the worst of all because it, like the fingers, was skinless, the vital organs spilling out of the rib cage, the intestines slipping out from behind the stomach and the liver hanging by a few weak blood vessels near the pelvic bones. The lungs shrivelled and blackened, though they were still, every now and then, let out rasping sounds, which almost constituted breathing. Then... there was the heart, a black ball no larger then a child's fist, which pumped the dark blue blood of the creature around its body, with the occasional squirt of the vile liquid out of holes in the heart.

The robber couldn't tear his eyes away from the sight. The circle of light now held him, with electric bolts connecting him to the sphere of electricity. He felt it then, a sweeping tiredness that engulfed him. He staggered backwards into the shelf where the candle stood and, with scrambling fingers, he tried to grip it but, as his fingertips touched it, he was hit by another wave of tiredness and his flailing hands made the candle wobble and tilt until, after what felt like an eternity, it fell onto the robber's body.

As the fire hit the ball of light it became a fireball with its screaming victim trapped inside. No matter how hard he hit and scratched at the fiery walls, he couldn't escape. Through the flames he saw the corpse standing just above him with its hand stretched out towards the flames and, even as he watched this, the robber felt his life force ebbing away.

The corpse, however, was changing. It was growing, bones mending, skin growing back, so that when the transformation was completed the robber found himself looking at a mirror image of himself. He opened his mouth to voice unknown words but couldn't, all he could feel was a piercing pain all over his body and, as he watched, his skin shrivelled, his legs contorted and, before his very eyes, his body aged into the same living skeleton he had seen lying in the coffin.

The white light vanished, as did the flames, and the ring slipped off the bone of his finger and dropped to the floor with a clatter. Now the two men were silent, one with pain and terror, one with amusement. The thing, now looking exactly as his victim had before he had placed the ring on his finger, strolled over to where the terrified robber lay and slowly picked him up and carried him over to the coffin, laying him inside it, lifting the lid from the floor and placing the heavy stone on the top of the coffin, sealing the robber into his fate.

Finally, he bent down and picked up the ring from where it had rolled and went to place it on his finger, but thought better of it and retrieved the golden cup from the shelf where the robber had thrust it before, placing the ring inside it. The ring flashed.

"Don't worry, you'll be human again soon enough." Then it smiled at the ring, placing the cup gently back on the shelf and exiting the crypt the same place he had entered 300 years ago, turning as he did to seal the crypt and block out the muffled screams of terror before turning and vanishing into the dark night.

Undercover
by Oliver Vokes-Tilley aged 12

Name: Star McGuire
Age: 14 years old
Address: 12 James Road, Chesterfield
Occupation: Undercover Journalist

The sound of the trigger being pulled will never fade.

12th June 2000
A woman came to me after school asking me if I wanted to become an undercover journalist. I recognised her, she was head of the school newspaper and I was the main storywriter. I took the job and then found out I was starting the very next day and my big scoop was the sniper attacks that have been targeting the local youth club.

14th June 2000
Stopped Sniper!!
Yesterday a brand new journalist managed to name and shame the one and only Tableside sniper which has been targeting young and innocent youths. One of the many people who attend this club said, "We are all too scared to walk home and then one of our friends got injured so it made it even worse."
The snipping shows that I came through with the big story, everyone was wondering who had named and shamed the sniper. I said nothing.

17th June 2000

A different woman came up to me today, when I was working, and said I had caused too much trouble so I was fired. I pleaded and pleaded for another chance but she said NO!

18th June 2000

Undercover Sacked

The brand new journalist has been sacked for causing too much trauma and havoc in and around RND (royal news depot). The person has also ruined people's lives after they had recovered.

This is a cutting from today's paper. It really upset me.

20th June 2000

Sniper Breaks Out!!

21st June 2000

I have to go out some day. No, I will stay indoors. No. Yes. NO. YES!! I then gave in, I had to go. As I walked out the door I wondered where to go, to the park, the shops and then I thought, the youth club. BIG MISTAKE. When it was closing time (10:45) I was last out as usual but the only different thing was I heard a whisper, "Now". Click, the sound of the trigger being pulled will never fade. The bullet got me on the back of my leg. I just screamed. I crawled back to the youth club, it was locked. I just lay there and cried.

The Assassin
by Rachael Kells aged 14

It's late. The moon, full and fat, is blindingly bright through the window above her study. It's not a comforting light. It only makes the wide night sky seem even blacker. She shivers as she feels its icy breath wash over her sweating skin. Drawing the curtains swiftly, she settles back to her work.

The car grinds steadily to a halt. The window open, greedily drinking in the humid summer air. He fumbles for his lighter. As he flicks it on, his face is revealed, twisted and contorted with hate. Despite his pain you can see he is a handsome man, his ebony hair framing his worn face. His eyes, dark and calculating like a panther about to strike, conceal his inner torment.

He stares out of the window, surveying the house. It stands with the other houses like toy soldiers on parade. The postage stamp garden is overgrown, a mass of tangled weeds, neglected for more important work. His malevolent eyes are drawn to her study, a beacon of light piercing the blanket of darkness. He senses her.

She types angrily with passion, a stack of papers already beside her. Her pale skin is blanched until almost translucent from too many hours in front of the monitor. Too many hours dedicated to their cause. As the deadline approaches rapidly, the enormity of what she is doing finally sinks in.

He eases the door open and walks gravely to the rear of the car. Discarding his cigarette he crushes the embers with destructive ease. He reaches into the cavernous boot and picks it up. The metal seems to wriggle and try to escape his grasp, begging him to give up and go home. Warning him. He continues towards the house, even more determined than before, trying to submerge his feelings. The front door lets out its tell-tale creak, a noise he was not expecting and she knew only too well.

She looks up sharply. Her heart booms in her ears. Beating harder and harder, faster and faster. The hairs on the back of her neck rise as, from her window, she observes the unfamiliar car loitering menacingly outside. She strains her ears but hears nothing more. Her breathing slows as she returns to her desk and hastily clicks print.

He moves quickly now, gliding through the house. He pauses as his eyes become accustomed to the eerie mid light. He smells her perfume hanging in the air, sweet and sickly, just like her. Silently, he climbs the stairs, stealthy as a fox. He sees the light curling round the edges of the doorframe. He can hear movement. He grasps the door handle and squeezes gently.

She stands in front of him, staring. She does not flinch. She stands as if she knew he was coming and for what purpose. Their gazes lock, echoing between them.

"I'm sorry," he whispers. He closes his eyes and pulls the trigger. She gasps as the life evaporates from her body.

A single sheaf of paper drops from the printer, containing her final mortal words. He hesitates momentarily then retrieves it.

For three years I have been fighting for freedom. For three years I have been fighting for equality. For three years I have been fighting for justice. As man's fate should not be decided by the colour of his skin alone. Why do we persecute these people and condemn them as inferior when they are just the same as you or I? I urge you to examine your conscience and remember...
"*The peoples of the world must unite or they will surely perish...*"

His brow furrows. His hatred of himself now revealed as a single tear rolls silently down his face and falls silently on to the page. He shreds the words that will never be heard in his despondent hands. His black hands.

End Of The Line
by Shannon Gilmore aged 12

Crack! Lightning streaked across the sky. Rain poured down with such force that it was bouncing off the floor. But still the train hurtled forwards. Inside it a young, handsome man was asleep. An old, plump woman walked into the carriage, dragging a refreshments cart behind her.

"Refreshments?" she squealed shrilly. The man jumped awake, knocking his half empty coffee onto the floor.

"Oh, sorry," the lady gurgled as she wiped it off the table and seat with a napkin.

"I didn't realise that you were asleep," she said, although the expression on her face made it quite clear that she had.

"Would you like to replace it?" she asked sheepishly.

"No thanks," said the man coldly. She walked out of the carriage looking smug.

Twenty-seven year old Robby Mulholand swept back his longish black hair. He then rubbed the sleep out of his eyes before checking his designer Rolex watch that his girlfriend had bought him. It was 11:07pm. The train was slowing down.

"This has to be my stop now," he thought to himself. "I've been on this stupid thing for over six hours." Over the speaker a muffled voice was saying something. All that he could work out were two things:

This stop was called Duffle Lane and definitely wasn't his.

The other was, to his horror, that he was the last passenger on the train and this was the end of the line. He grabbed his rucksack and jumped off onto the platform where the bellboy gave him his holdall. The train sped away as quick as the lightning that was streaking the sky yellow. In between these sudden flashes of light, the only light that he had was coming from an old fashioned lamppost that was giving off a feeble whiteish glow. From this he could just about make out that the old train station was Victorian. He walked up to the old, rotting, wooden door and knocked twice, praying that it was still open so that he could get inside, away from this dreadful storm. No one answered so he tried the handle. It opened slowly with a creak.

He entered, glad to be in the dryness of indoors. I would like to say the warmth, only it wasn't warm at all. He stepped back in time as he stepped through that door (not literally). Into a world where there was no electricity and the only light came from a log and coal fire that was becoming very dim as it slowly burned itself out in the corner. He called out, "Hello! Can anyone hear me?"

The only reply was the daunting sound of his echo. He moved over to the other side of the room. There was a small ticket office. He tapped nervously on the shutter but, of course, no one picked it up. He walked round the staircase where he saw a huge, grand staircase. It was all wooden and varnished and set out like a real Victorian one. He stroked the wood and realised that it probably was Victorian.

Just then he heard some footsteps. He ran round the corner to see a man with wispy, grey hair leave through the oak door.

"Wait," he yelled, but then he noticed a hearing aid in the man's ear. He was deaf. Before he even had chance to wave his arms or get himself noticed, the old man had shut the door and Robby heard a key turn in the rusty lock. The caretaker had left for the night. Panicking, Robby grabbed his mobile from his pocket.

"Damn," he cried. No reception was receivable down here. Robby didn't know what to do, but he knew that he had to do something. Pretty soon he gave up hope and decided that he'd just have to stay until it reopened in the morning. He cuddled by the fire so that he got maximum heat and light, but soon it was almost completely out. He decided that he'd have to get something to burn from somewhere and so (using the light from his phone) he made his way up the grand staircase.

At the top he found a room with a heap of papers and a glass case. The papers were old and dusty – the sort that school children often try to impersonate by coffee staining cartridge paper and burning the corners. Inside the glass case was a red cushion and, laid out for all to see, was a mouldy, green, human hand that was so disgusting that it sent shivers through his spine.

He flipped through the papers trying to find something that wasn't important so that he could burn it. He was just reading some boring documents when he came across something that looked interesting. It was a non-fiction story entitled 'The Railway Murderer'. This is how it went.

The Railway Murderer

Seventeen years ago, on the 19/12, a terrible murder took place. Well, to be precise, five murders on five different trains. Each time the victim died in the same way and then was thrown out of the door and found at the bottom of the slope on the opposite side of the railway track than Duffle Lane station. All of these murders were on females – pregnant females. There was one major link between the DNAs of the bodies – they all showed that the unborn babies had the same dad.

The murders were executed perfectly and not a fingerprint was found. Except in the fifth one where something went seriously wrong. In the first four the murderer had left the vehicle at Duffle Lane. But he was seen in the fifth one and a lady screamed not to let him off. So the driver quickly snapped the doors shut. He was fast but not fast enough. The man escaped alive and untagged but missing his right hand.

The police had used the DNA to find police records of the man and many people and officers have searched for him. But there has only ever been one sighting of him which was at Duffle Lane railway station on the 19/12 thirteen years ago. Police guessed that he has changed his name (originally James Robertson) and has moved abroad, probably to Spain.

Underneath this story there was a picture of the man. It was a horrifying sight. A young man about Robby's age but certainly not as handsome as Robby. He had yellowish, pale, waxy skin stretched out over thin, high cheekbones. His blonde, straw like hair hung low over his face, so much so that you couldn't see his eyes. It was the 18/12 the day that Robby had got off the train. Somewhere in the distance he heard a church's bells chime twelve times. It was midnight and the days had turned. It was now the 19/12 – the precise day of the railway murder and the only ever sighting of the murderer since.

Robby had heard enough. He grabbed some papers and ran downstairs where he built up a roaring fire.

"I'm not going to let those stories get to me," he told himself. As hard as he tried, they did. The fear was a big, black, hungry dog which ate at his mind and nerves until he was so scared that he wouldn't even turn around in case he saw the murderer.

Slowly, one by one, the hours ticked by until, finally, he heard the church bells chime seven times and then the sound of a key turning in the rusty lock and the creak of the door as it swung open on its rusty hinges. He jumped up and gathered his stuff ready to catch the first train out of there, when the man who'd opened the door walked in. He was short and stumpy and had headphones in his ears. He did a groovy little dance over to the ticket box (singing aloud) where he pulled out a key. At that moment, he noticed Robby and jumped literally two feet in the air with shock.

"You scared me to death," he cried in a deep voice with a Newcastle accent. Robby went through the whole story of how he'd got stuck there and the man let him go.

"Boy am I glad to be out of that place," he said to himself, so happy that he was talking aloud. Just then he saw a man who he recognised faintly from somewhere. He must have noticed Robby looking at him because he raised his left hand and gave his hat a touch in a formal greeting. Robby then saw that the man had no right hand, just a stub! He screamed and ran across a nearby field. He turned and his heart missed a beat when he saw that the man wasn't even chasing him. He slowed down a touch, but then a mouldy, green hand came up out of the soil. It clasped tightly around his ankle and began to pull him underground...

Phase 1
by Grace Smith aged 12

Two years ago, the Abromwitz family were the happiest people on their street. Then, with the sudden death of Mrs Abromwitz, the family lay in ruins. Jane, the family nanny, became the glue that held the family together. Over time, Mr Abromwitz fell in love with Jane. One year ago, Jane became the second Mrs Abromwitz and everything seemed perfect and everybody seemed happy again.

"Hurry up Tiffany, it's time to go," shouted Tiffany's stepmother. Tiffany was the last one ready as usual. Tiffany looked very much like her mother with long, dark hair and big, brown eyes. She was tall for her age, 13, she had inherited her height from her father and her features from her mother.

Andrew and Harriet were already arguing over who was going to sit in the front of the car on the way to school. "Both of you are too young to sit in the front so stop arguing now," Jane told them.

Andrew and Harriet were identical twins. They both had hazel eyes like their father and dark hair like their mother. They both were 5 and very noisy for their size. Everything went quiet, then Tiffany walked down the stairs as if nothing was wrong.

"Hurry up, we're going to be late," Jane shouted.

Today was the day Phase 1 of the Abromwitz children's master plan was to take action.

The children disliked Jane and decided to make a plan to drive her away. Phase 1 of their master plan was to prevent Jane from getting to her 'big business meeting' she had been getting excited about for the past three weeks. The plan was to unplug her alarm clock which they had already done and failed at. The next step was for the twins to argue, tantrum and completely ignore Jane which was now about to happen.

"It's my turn," screamed Andrew.

"NO IT'S NOT," yelled Harriet at the top of her voice. Mrs Harrison from number 5 was walking her dog and stopped to observe this slanging match.

"Sorry for all the noise," said Jane, Mrs Harrison nodded and carried on with her walk.

"STOP IT NOW!" shouted Jane competing in the match.

As planned the twins completely ignored her and began pulling each other's hair.

"Ooowwwww," yelped Andrew in pain.

"You shouldn't have pulled my hair, big ears," bellowed Harriet in reply.

By this time, the twins had made enough noise to attract the whole row who were now watching the wrestling match from their windows and caused Jane much embarrassment. Her second attempt was to lure them away from each other with lollies. But they remembered the words that their faithful leader had told them, and ignored Jane. Harriet then decided to push

Andrew over, causing him to fall on his head and crack it open. Jane spent the rest of the day in A&E, missed her meeting, and Phase 1 was complete.

Under The Lake
by Richard Peters aged 11

Everything seemed to happen so quickly that night, it was too fast for him to bear. He felt like he was going to explode.

Anyway, let me start at the beginning. There were five of us that night, all grouped together in the tent I bought at the corner shop only days before, not knowing what would happen to it on our camp. We set up everything at around 4:30, leaving enough time to explore the area around the base, as we called it, and maybe further into the wilderness.

Steve and I were first to scan the terrain from in the tent, the other three, Mick, Simon and Olli were practising with the weapons we brought, hopefully we wouldn't need to use them, but I had a bad feeling about the bubbling lake right next to us.

Steve, of course, was cool as a cucumber. "Don't worry Darren, nothing's going to happen," Steve said when I told him about my fears. I wasn't so sure but I shut up anyway.

Suddenly, something large and skull shaped flew into the tent. I had to jump to my left to avoid the spinning object hitting me in the face. "See!" I roared at Steve.

"There's something in there waiting for a moment to strike us down and throw our skulls at other unlucky campers who will come here!" Olli and Simon tried and, in the end, succeeded in calming me down. I was really annoyed at Steve because he looked as placid as ever. He didn't even flinch when the skull flew in, he just sat staring blankly at the floor not even listening to me rant at him.

He soon snapped back into action and was telling us his plan to rid the lake of whatever was in it; the plan contained self-sacrifice and teamwork. The five of us always worked together in sports and schoolwork so we had that on our side, but we knew nothing about the beast and probably wouldn't unless we killed it.

We stood getting our weapons ready and preparing mentally for the task ahead. Mick was best prepared, he had three kitchen knives and a metal bin lid he could use as a shield. I, of course, was worst off with only a child's samurai sword to defend myself. The others had an array of knives, picks and chisels.

"Ready you lot?" said Mick, holding two of his knives ready, the third in his pocket and the bin lid on his back.

"Ready." Was the reply from all of us.

When we walked outside, it wasn't hard to tell the beast was waiting. The water was as still as a millpond, the calm before the storm, every second watching, waiting, each side wanting the other to strike first. Steve threw a small chisel into the water. It must have found its target because there was a screech of pain from below the water. In answer, the beast launched a tentacle at Steve's leg. He smacked it away calmly and yanked his chisel out. Then, with a deadly and accurately placed throw, the chisel sunk deep into the creature's lower jaw. It roared in pain and sent a tentacle flying for Olli's head. "Olli, duck!" I screamed, but it was too late. With a smash, Olli's crushed skull fell to the floor followed closely by his body. A large pool of blood was spilling out from his neck and tinting the floor crimson.

Using the moment of shock to its advantage, the beast struck again, this time through Simon's ribcage. Its screech in triumph was cut short by my sword going through its belly. It wrenched away leaving me unarmed. I dived to my right and picked up Simon's two picks, gasping for breath like a new born calf. I saw my chance when Mick joined the battle. He was fighting like a hardened warrior alongside Steve.

I crept round the back of the beast and drove both picks into the back of its neck…

"Time for bed boys!" called a shrill voice from downstairs.

"Don't argue with your mother lads," I said before they started pleading. "Hey, I'll tell you more tomorrow night and remember, it's all true!" I pressed with an edge to my voice. "But, don't, tell, your, mother." I grinned savagely and left.

I Knew He Was Coming
by Amiee Bamford aged 11

I knew he was coming, I could see him, I could hear him from miles away, but I was the only one who could. I knew he would come, he said, he promised he would. He would come and stand next to me with a piece of paper with an address on it. I knew that he wanted me to go to this place to kill the person who killed him, then I would have two graves to look at, not just one. Just at that moment, the paper that I'd been waiting for floated down beside my feet. I stood there silently staring at where the paper had landed, then I picked it up, I felt a shiver up my spine, then he flew off.

I knew I had to do it, so I started walking in the direction of what the paper told me to, all the way down Chapel Road to the dead end. There was the house; I stepped through the gate, up the three stairs and through the creaky door. There he was, I walked up to him, my heart was beating so fast that I thought it would just pop out. There was a knife on the side, I picked it up, and he had something in his hand too. I put my hand up ready to stab him, he followed me, he did exactly what I did. My hand went forward so fast that I didn't know what had happened. Did I kill him? I then felt a sting in my stomach. I looked down, he was gone, then I looked down even more and I found something sticking in me, I didn't kill him, he had killed me.

Mrs Meteor

by Daniel Fawley aged 12

Tuesday 28th May 1999

I am Jeff Spray and I have just discovered a meteor hurtling towards Earth. From my calculations, the meteor should hit around June 8th to June 18th.

8th June 1999

The small meteor should enter the Earth's atmosphere and hit the English Channel somewhere between Dover and Calais. The government has sent word to evacuate Dover and the French have been informed to evacuate Calais.

10th June 1999

The meteor is due to hit today. I will be monitoring its position from here in my Scottish chalet. I hope there will be no injuries, but I have done my best to secure this devastation by having three families staying with me in a seven man chalet. But what is this? The meteor is changing course – there is no predicting where it will hit now.

At the same time on June 10th an old woman was crossing the road in Manchester when an armoured car ran her over without a care in the world. The old woman was knocked on the floor. The police car came speeding around the corner and, only having a quick glimpse of the old woman on the floor, the police officer slammed his brakes on but it was too late. The old woman was run over a second time. Someone called an ambulance and, about five minutes later, it turned up. As the paramedics lifted her into the ambulance, a green, supersonic, glowing light shot into her wound and immediately healed the skin. But the paramedics could only guess the green light and healing powers were the meteor that was supposed to hit the English Channel.

When she found she had special powers she used them to fight evil.

Scary Seas
by Lauren Brown aged 13

Chapter 1

The wave breaks at my feet and I remember that time, long ago, I wish was all forgotten. The sun is rising in the distance and I need to get home, but I still cannot forget what happened and it is still clear in my mind from 16 years ago. Why do we still live here? Why can't I leave this dreaded place? My family tell me all the time we are too poor, but I can't live here anymore and I will tell you why you are the only people that know the truth.

I will take you back, 16 years ago, to the year 1987.

I was a young boy at the time. My name is Jeremy Plain and I live in St Ives in Cornwall. I have done all my life.

Chapter 2

When I was a little boy my friends dared me to, well,

175

push a young girl in the water as a joke, but I didn't have the courage to do it so I said to them that they only wanted me to do it because they didn't want to get into trouble. I turned and headed down the cliff home. When I looked back to see if they were still there, a man pushed me and the little girl down the cliff. He, as I found out later in life, was a mad man and he had heard my friends telling me to push the girl so he did instead.

As we reached the sea I swam as fast as I could to reach the girl. She told me her name was Jessica and that she was scared. I grabbed hold of her and tried to pull her to shore. Then a boat approached us and we shouted and shouted but the fisherman just said, "Stupid kids, when their parents find out they are jumping in the deep sea... not my problem."

The man just sped off and left us. I found some left over energy from inside and swam to the shore. It would have been easy if Jessica wasn't weighing me down. It was pretty scary. At first I thought I was going to drown but I got used to the extra weight after a while. Then disaster struck again. A storm was brewing out at sea and sea storms that time of year are very nasty. I swam with all my power until I reached the cliff.

Chapter 3

The cliff base was at least safer than in the middle of the sea, well at least a little safer. As the sun was going down, it was getting more dangerous at the cliff than I had expected. The sea was lapping up at our feet and Jessica was getting more scared than before as the water was splashing up at our waists. I took hold of Jessica and swam into the sea. I could see the beach from where I was and I put all my power into reaching my target of getting there.

When I finally got to the beach, I dragged Jessica up the beach and looked down at her and smiled but the gentle, black, shiny hair and the sparkling, blue eyes were not happy – they stood still and, at that moment, I knew the worst had occurred.

She was dead.

So now that is why I dread the sea and that is why the entire town think I killed Jessica. The only people that believe me are my family and the police.

Hunted
by Alex Muir aged 13

Roan paced slowly across the kitchen floor. Where was Boww? He should have been back hours ago. A creak behind him distracted him from his thoughts. His younger brother, Isaac, was climbing into a chair.

"Isaac, you should be asleep. What are you doing up?"

"Isn't Da back yet?"

"No. I'm beginning to worry. He's never stayed out this late before." He turned to the window, looking out at the black mass that was the woods.

Da had gone out that morning, hunting in the woods as he always did, once a month. He had promised to be back before nightfall but, even about three hours after the sun had set, he still hadn't come home.

Turning back to his brother, Roan announced, "I'm going out to look for him."

"What about me and Leena?" queried Isaac.

"I'll call in at Mrs Herball's, she should still be up."

"What do I do until she comes?"

"Just make sure your sister doesn't wake up and don't do anything dangerous."

"Ok, good luck finding Da," called Isaac, already halfway down the corridor.

Roan began gathering his things together. He collected his pack and filled it with provisions, then he filled his water skin from the well. This done, he shouldered his bow, checked his supply of arrows, made sure his knife was in his belt and finally checked his brother was doing as he had asked. Isaac had already fallen back to sleep. Oh well, he would just have to hope nothing happened until he had fetched Mrs Herball.

Roan's cabin was just on the edge of the village, only about quarter of a mile away from the woods. Da had built it himself with the help of a few of the village men. His mother had passed away a few months later, much to the distress of everyone in the village as she had made friends with most, if not all, of them.

When he got to Mrs Herball's, Roan explained the

situation to Mrs Herball (the village healer). She said she would be happy to help.

Once he had made sure everything was fine at home, Roan set off.

Only a few people entered the woods, as rumours were passed around that the trees sometimes came alive and attacked travellers that strayed off the path. As a result, only hunters, travellers and the plain stupid entered the wood, though only a few of those had encountered abnormalities.

As Roan entered, a shiver ran down his spine. Now he could see how the rumours were formed. The trees had grown close together, the trunks never more than a metre apart. A thin mist swirled in eddies around his leather-clad feet, sometimes cloaking them from view. The light wind moving between the trees made a moaning that could easily be mistaken for the call of a supernatural creature. Looking around he could see no sign of Da. It looked like he would have to go deeper.

He had only been into the woods once before but he had been too young to remember anything about it. Da had said that he had only been in there a few seconds before he had run out again, scared.

After walking for about half an hour and after having to light his torch, Roan still hadn't found Da or anything that might suggest where he was. He needed some help. He was just about to turn around and get some of the other hunters from the village to help him when he heard a change in the moaning. There was now a deeper moan resonating along with the wind. Roan shifted his torch, knocked an arrow into his bow and began to follow the sound. He kept his breathing light, just in case the owner of the noise meant him harm. As he passed by a tree, the moaning suddenly ceased. He twisted around pulling his bowstring taught. Then seeing what had been making the noise, he relaxed the bowstring and tossed down his bow before racing forward to aid Da. A snapped arrow shaft was lying next to Da's shoulder where his rough deerskin jacket was split and stained with red. Roan raised his torch to Da's pallid face. Da's breathing was shallow and when Roan tried to help him up his face contorted with pain.

After inspecting the wound which was rather shallow, Roan bandaged it up and asked what had happened.

"I won't go into too much detail because we can't stay here long, there's something dangerous out there," exclaimed Da, "but here's what happened. I was tracking a deer buck so I had strayed off the track." Roan nodded, listening intently. Da shifted himself into a more comfortable position, then continued. "It was around midday when the deer buck entered a clearing to graze with deer packs that were resting there. I was about to attack it when all the deer leaped up and bolted. When I turned around this arrow hit me in the shoulder. Whoever fired it had a bad shot; there was enough force in the arrow to knock me off my feet so they must have been close. All I remember after that is trying to reach the path so I would be easier to find."

Roan looked at the arrow properly for the first time. It was very crude, it was just a carved stick with a single feather to help it fly. It didn't even have an arrowhead. "Luckily I managed to pull it out before I fell, otherwise I wouldn't be here," grimaced Da. "Who did you leave Isaac and Leena with anyway?"

"Mrs Herball."

"Good, she'll look after them well."

There was a sudden crack of a twig.

"Grab your pack and move!" hissed Da, "I'll be right behind you."

Silently, they made their way along the woodland path, clambering over rocks and logs. They were metres from the edge of the trees when a great barrier of chopped wood loomed up in front of them.

A leaf crunched behind them.

"Quick! Follow me," gasped Da and dodged between the trees on the side of the path. As Roan followed him he heard the distant crash of water. After climbing a short rise, Da halted unexpectedly. Roan only just managed to stop before he knocked Da over the edge of a shallow canyon with a fast flowing river coursing along its bottom. After checking for a place to forge, and finding none, Boww came to a conclusion. "We'll have to try and jump."

"What! I can't jump that far!"

"You'll have to. Look, I'll go first." Da backed up slightly then ran and pushed off. He landed on the far bank, five or so metres away. All doubts Roan had vanished with the rustling of a bush behind him. He backed up then launched himself off the edge. As he looked up, the far wall came rising up to meet him. He dropped his torch, but the lack of trees around the canyon allowed the moon to shine through and him to see a firm hand gripping his wrist. He glanced up to see Da pulling him up with his good arm.

When he was safely on the other side of the canyon, Roan looked up at Da's pained face.

"Thank you," he managed to gasp.

"No problem," grinned Da.

Looking back across the canyon, they could see the mysterious figure standing on the other side. It was garbed in green and had its hood up covering its face. It backed up, getting ready to jump. As it launched itself off the edge, its hood snagged on something and it tumbled down towards the river, letting out an angry wail.

"Let's go," said Boww putting his arm around Roan's shoulders and turning from the canyon.

When they left the wood they discovered that the river had been flowing into the wood and was one that they actually knew and also had a forging point allowing them to cross and make their way back to the village.

By the time they got into well known territory, dawn had broken and, as they made their way across the meadow on the outskirts of the village, two familiar figures appeared, running, outlined against the rising sun.

"Da!" chorused Leena and Isaac closing ground quickly.

"I'm back!" replied Boww hurrying forward to meet them with Roan not far behind.

Tom's Tragic Tale
by Anthony Newington aged 11

Boo! Ha scared you already and the true horror of this utterly tragic tale hasn't even began to unfold yet. If you whimper when you go upstairs at night or wince at the mere thought of dark red blood oozing out of someone's body, then put this book in a military safe and throw it into the deepest, darkest part of the sea. This grim tale has more blood, petrified people and disasters than anything you will ever have read. So either burn this book or endure the frights within!

I don't really know how it all started but I'll try my best to describe it, I'm sure you won't understand however hard I try, but here I go... oh sorry, I forgot to introduce myself. My name's Tom Taylor and I'm a twelve year old who lives in the heart of Manchester. Now let my tragic tale begin.

It was a normal Monday in normal Manchester and everything was perfectly normal. The sound of thousands of normal people's feet could be heard hurrying around as normal. I was walking past a toyshop and glanced into the window... what I saw was definitely not normal! There was a boy about the same height as me, staring right into my eyes. I noticed that on his right arm there were gashes with blood oozing out. I looked to see if there were any on his left arm but he had no left arm! Instead, where his arm should have joined to his torso, there was a bone sticking out, also oozing with dark, cherry red blood. The sight made me feel sick but the boy looked familiar. The expression on his face made him look petrified or frozen with fear. I looked around me to see if anyone else had noticed him, but everyone was just rushing around like normal. I turned my attention back to the boy but he was gone, instead there was my own reflection staring back at me. I must have just imagined him.

When I got home that evening I didn't mention anything strange to my Mum but couldn't stop thinking about the expression on that boy's face. He looked so helpless with his pale eyes wide open in fear and mouth that seemed to be screaming. Suddenly, my Dad burst through the door, scaring the life out of me and my Mum. He was beaming ear to ear and started singing while also telling us that he had won the work's lottery. He had won first prize which was a luxury cruise around the world! I was so giddy I couldn't keep my legs still – I had never been further south than Stockport. I jumped onto the table and started dancing. My Mum didn't really care that I was crushing all the plates, she was too busy hugging and kissing my Dad.

It was the night before the ship set sail and we were packing our bags into the car. It was a chilly night and the wind howled like a wolf through the trees. Even though the weather was lousy, I was still as giddy as a week before when we first got the fantastic news. I hopped into the back seat and we set off on our long journey to Brighton port. Rain threw itself at the window of our Ford Escort, but on the horizon I could see the sun just peaking over the hills.

By the time we reached the port, the sun had come out but the rain was still pouring down on us. We lined up, gave our ticket to the man in the small yellow kiosk and stepped into the magnificent ship.

The main hall was about twice the size of my house and gold patterns ran circles around the ceiling. The floor was made of marble and, because it had just been polished, it was dangerously slippy. Marble pillars stretched up from the floor to the ceiling, forming a circle in the centre of the hall.

I had a 1st class cabin all to myself and my parents shared one right next door to mine. When I opened the door I was overwhelmed by the quality of what I saw. There was a four poster bed in the middle of the bedroom with an oak bedside table. I jumped on the bed and sank right into the ultra-comfy mattress. The main room of my cabin had a thirty-two inch plasma TV with Sky+, a DVD player and a video player. Facing the TV was a four person leather sofa and a reclining leather armchair. My cabin had no kitchen because, on the ship, there was a five star restaurant which served all kinds of food from around the world. The bathroom was the best bit because there was an enormous bath with a built-in Jacuzzi, a power shower which automatically turned itself on and off when you placed your hand over a sensor and a toilet and sink that were also operated by sensors.

The storm had already started when we left the port. By the time we got to open water it was quite fierce. I was in the restaurant with my parents, eating some strange food from India, when I was disturbed by jolts of the ship. I went to my cabin to get some rest. I must have fallen asleep. I woke to a sound, a crunching, scraping sound. The hull on the starboard side had hit a rock that jutted out from the sea bed. Darkness. Pitch black. I could hear the ship creaking and straining. I could hear screams and smell fear in the air. I looked to my window... darkness, but I could hear the rain and see it dripping down the pane. Then that creaking again, like a cat being tormented.

I don't know how but I managed to get on deck. I kept on slipping. The deck was waterlogged. The ship was sinking. All the life boats were already full with women and their screaming children. I followed my instinct and jumped into the blackness of the whirling sea below.

I fell for what seemed like an eternity then… it was so cold. I opened my eyes but it was black. I tried to reach what I thought was the surface but I couldn't. I struggled against tonnes of black, black water. Something stung my right arm. By the time I did reach the surface all my energy had been drained out of me and the smell of blood was everywhere. Something big, something very big brushed past my legs but I couldn't see a thing. It was either the coldness of the water or pure fear, but whatever it was it ran up my back and froze my brain. I couldn't move a muscle. All around me I could hear people screaming. The smell of blood increased to a sickening stench and the pain in my arm became unbearable. I tried to call for help but only a tiny squeak managed to escape my mouth.

The sky suddenly lit up as the once magnificent ship exploded, sending bits of debris shooting out into the sea. A small piece of wood hit me in the head and almost knocked me unconscious. The last thing I remember after that was two rows of giant shining teeth appearing out of nowhere…

I woke up in hospital and couldn't feel my left arm. A nurse came into my ward with a very concerned look on her face. She walked over to my bed and kneeled down next to me. She told me I had been found lying unconscious a few miles away on the Brighton beach. My left arm had been ripped off, possibly by a shark, and deep gouges had been dug into my right arm, also suspected to be done by a shark. If they hadn't found me then there would have been no hope that even surgery would have kept me alive. The hospital had identified me. Apparently my Mum had been torn apart by a shark and her mangled body, barely recognisable, was found a few miles west of mine. They didn't know what had happened to my Dad but they expected he was lost at sea.

All that month I was in most of the headlines, being one of only a few survivors of the terrible accident. Now I'm stuck here in this grotty children's home, my fame over but wounds still intact. I now know that the boy in the toyshop window was me! I'm writing about my tragic accident, hoping to earn enough money to start a new life of my own. If you are reading this sentence it probably means that you have bought my book. That's another fiver to me. Thanks a lot!

The Werewolf
by Elliot Garlick aged 11

It was a chilly, more than depressing night. The wind was howling through the streets, rattling and screaming like a ghoul trapped in a cage. That was when it all began…

I never have been a 'normal' boy, I admit. I've been a bit dim at times. I admit I was never perfect. But what happened to me, well, not a single person in the past, present or future deserves it. Not a single soul. But life, it's like that. Yeah, some people would argue, "There's always two sides to a story." They could say, "I told you not to go into the woods at night." But whenever someone denies you the right to do something, it makes you want to do that same thing even more!

So, it was one Halloween they dared me. By 'they' I mean Tom Pritchett, his father was a professional boxer, Liam Bowlan, chairperson of the school council, and Jake Noble, his father was a politician. And it wasn't just any dare. Everyone who had teased and frightened and bullied me through my first year at high school wouldn't be able to call me 'scaredy cat' or chant, "Mike Bruiser is a loser!" So I took the dare. But I didn't choose to become… well, what I did. That's just not the kind of guy I am. I don't take things lying down. So, here's how it happened…

The actual dare was to stay in the Bowstring Wood until midnight. But, you should know, every single VAMPIRE, UFO and WEREWOLF that any drunk or hobo had ever 'spotted' would always be connected to the wood. You should also know that I have been terrified of the wood for more years than I'd care to count. And the bullies that dared me knew this. So I chose to try and show them that they couldn't boss me or anyone else around anymore. I tried to be a hero. I didn't know what I'd let myself in for. So, true to my word, I slowly descended into the forest. I began to realise what I had gotten myself into. I'd only really accepted it on the spur of the moment.

As I thought about the horrifying and gory stories that came out of those woods, I thought about the whiplash vampire that drained its victims of not only their blood, but of every bodily fluid. He then dumped their carcasses on their doorstep (it is true that dead bodies have been appearing on doorsteps since, well, a long time ago). After about ten minutes, I eventually found a clearing that would suit my purpose well. It had a small log that would be just right for sitting and waiting. I checked my watch, I only had ten more minutes longer to wait. I sat and stared around for a short while and checked my watch again. Five minutes, did something just rustle behind me? Four minutes, three, two, one (last minute!). Only five seconds... four... three... two... one... zero! I'd done it! I tried to conquer my fear and I did it! A solemn bell rang in the distance. I stopped dead in my tracks. I was sure I'd just heard something. I spun and checked again. That was my first big mistake. A gigantic, hairy shape leaped on my back. That night I remember that I screamed bloody murder...

It slashed open my back. I cried in agony. It bit into the flesh of my neck. I stumbled. My foot lashed out on its own accord and caught it in the stomach. Confused at the loss of its prey, the thing was completely off guard. I fell and gave a tremendous death snarl. As I caught the final glimpse into the creature's eyes I saw sorrow, anger, hatred and (no, it couldn't be... could it?) fear? It fell. There was a bloodcurdling howl. The thing fell back and impaled itself on a crudely sharpened branch. I just stood there, dumbstruck, staring at the size of it. It looked like a wolf, it smelt like a wolf, but it wasn't like any wolf I've ever seen. It was easily seven foot tall and reeked to heaven! I looked and I looked. Then I turned away, blinked and looked again. The wolf just wouldn't disappear. So I ran. I didn't know which direction. I didn't really care either. I just wanted to get away from that horrible, stinking corpse. Before I knew it, I was standing in front of my house. I felt so tired. Just so, so tired. I somehow managed to dig my key out of my pocket. I opened the door, staggered through the frame, then closed and locked the door behind me. I slithered up the stairs and into my bedroom. I fell into my bed. As soon as my head hit the pillow I was already in a deep and nauseous sleep.

I woke to the sound of my mother's voice screaming. I jumped to my feet. Although I couldn't recall the night before for a few seconds, it all came flooding back to me. A few hours later, my mum was holding a cup of coffee and a policeman was asking me if I recalled anything from the 'burglary'. That's what I said. That a thief broke into our house. Then he knocked me out and that was all I could remember. Well, what else would you say? "Oh, I was bitten by a huge wolf, I fought it and won." You'd be locked in a padded room wearing a straight jacket!

That night was a full moon. It was the most horrifying night of my entire life…

I woke up in the middle of the night. I felt hot. Too hot. I absentmindedly scratched the top of my head. "Man I need a hair cut," I thought out loud. I scratched my arm, "Jesus Christ!" I yelled. Or tried to. All that came out was a vicious snarl. I bounded up to my mirror. "Noooooooooooooooooooooo," I screamed. Or, to be more precise, howled. I tried to lean against the wall but, instead, put my hand through it! It was solid brick! There was a back alley near my house, I thought I'd sleep there for a night and try to make sense of all this in the morning. But they had different plans…

'They' were werewolves. Huge, beastly, horrible things. "You," spat one of them viciously, "you murdered our leader." You could practically hear venom writhing as he spoke.

"Yes," said another, "why?"

"Because…," I licked my lips and tried again, "because you're evil, you eat flesh. You kill people then eat them! You're cannibals! And he tried to murder me!" I managed to stammer.

"The boy thinks we're evil!" shouted one. They all laughed. If you can call a number of howls filling the night sky, laughter. "Maybe he did try to kill you," said the third, tears of laughter still in his eyes, "but we never eat more than our fill."

"But now you're one of us and there are so precious few of us, we don't kill our own," said the first.

"So...so what are you going to do to me now?" I enquired.

"We are going to do to you what we do to every single new werewolf that joins our ranks," said the second. "We are going to invest you."

"Take you under our wing," said the third.

"Teach you and show you the noble way of the werewolf," said the last.

"But first," said one, "you have to prove your worth and courage…"

"So, what do I have to do again?" I asked. It was the following night.

"It is quite simple really," said the eldest, "all you have to do is travel into the Bowstring Woods and do battle with the vampire that lives there."

"Right, all set?" said Vincent. I had recently learned all their names. The youngest was Vincent, at around three thousand years. The second youngest was Michelangelo (NOT the artist) at five thousand. And the oldest (at five thousand five hundred) was Thomas.

After what seemed like a lifetime, I nodded.

"Good," said Thomas, "the only rule is, the only way you can complete the test is to defeat the vampire. Oh, and one more thing. We do not want to resort to it but, if you try to run away, we will be forced to kill you." He said the last part as casually as you would mention the weather!

So, once again, I found myself unwillingly entering the forest. I walked for what seemed to be the best part of an hour. I eventually reached the clearing but it wasn't how I left it. It was as if a creature had been looking for something… or someone! There was a groan to my left. I backed away with a start. A man who was wearing the left over of what could have been pyjamas got up and stared at me. Not particularly frightening, just apparently curious. Then it smiled and bared its huge fangs. As quick as lightning it dived on me and tried to place a blow. I felt an unfamiliar anger take hold of me. I suddenly felt myself grow. And I don't mean a spurt. Every single inch of my body grew, including my teeth. Before, I was four foot two, now I was easily six foot and as mad as hell. And instead of having normal teeth, they grew about as long as a finger and as sharp as kitchen knives! It was time for the battle of the species to begin…

I thought it would be like an old monster movie. First we would trade insults, then the fight would start with small cuts and work up to the serious wounds. But it wasn't like that. The vampire was obviously shocked that I was a werewolf. To be honest, I was a little as well. I thought you could only turn werewolf when it was a full moon. I'd have to ask the others… if I survived! It dived at my throat, fangs poised, ready to bite into my flesh. My instincts kicked in. I rolled to the side and kicked him as he flew past. He was there, sprawled out in front of me. He also rolled to the side but I was ready. He got up and tried to head butt me but, swift as the vampire was, the fact was – I was swifter. Just as his head would have hit me, I grabbed it and twisted it cruelly to the left. The vampire made no sound. There was just a loud "CRACK" and I knew the vampire was dead. That was it. I'd won!

Just to make sure that the vampire was dead, I fastened him to the ground with some sturdy tree roots I found. I thought that if he was truly dead then he wouldn't be much trouble. And if he wasn't, well, he soon would be. So I joyfully ran through the woods, a strange scent met my nose. It was in-between a skunk and bad deodorant. I approached with the most extreme caution that I could muster after a long and tiring battle. And, after what I saw then, I couldn't even muster that much. There, in a silver cage, was Vincent and Michelangelo. But where was Thomas? Then (unfortunately) I saw him. But there was a man. He looked like he hadn't had a shower in weeks. But he bore a look in his eyes that told me he'd been waiting for this moment for a very, very long time…
To be continued…

Meant To Be (Part One)
by Matthew Hockey aged 17

I – Frank (Two Days Ago)

After a few moments listening to the sound of an empty line, Frank gently put the phone back in its cradle. A tear slid quietly from the corner of his eye. It wasn't so much what they had talked about on the phone that had upset him. It's what they hadn't. Or, more accurately, what he hadn't been able to bring himself to say.

"I like you."

"I love you."

"I need you."

"I want you."

He'd always wanted to do it, he always meant to do it. To just break the cycle of their words and drop the bombshell. But the sound of her voice always stopped him in his tracks. It was a beautiful voice filled with happiness and life. How sad it would be, Frank always thought, to hear that voice raised in anger. April only had sweet words and kind thoughts for him. So he knew how soul crushing it would be to hear her say, "Urgh, get away from me you freak!" or even worse, "How long have we been friends now Frank and you spring this on me, I never want to see you again."

Frank could all too easily imagine her saying those things. All the possible scenarios ran through his head, causing his gut to tighten and his diaphragm to lock. When he tried to speak, all that came out was a dry squeak. She always assumed that it was a bad connection, a problem with the line. She had no idea of the inner turmoil he faced every time they spoke.

Frank sat up straight in his chair, realising he'd been staring at the phone for a full ten minutes. He needed something else to occupy his mind, he wheeled himself over to the CD player and flicked on his favourite track. Frank turned to his low shelves, he couldn't reach anything higher. That's where he kept his pictures. There was one of April, it was a copy of her graduation photo, she'd looked beautiful that day. But to Frank, that was no different to any other day. She seemed to look more beautiful every time he saw her. He often wondered if other people saw her the way he did and, if so, why weren't there more crashes when they walked down the street. He winced at the thought of a car accident.

II – April (Two Days Ago)

After saying her farewells, she pressed the disconnect button on her speaker phone. April hated ending their phone calls, she always got the feeling that there was something he wasn't saying. She felt that he'd say it if she just gave him room. He never did, he just went on hiding it. At first she'd thought it was kind of interesting, he had an air of mystery about him. But after a while it just got a bit strange. She got by. She'd known Frank for quite a long time, since university in fact. His graduation picture was up on the mantelpiece with his riding shotgun. The pictures were a testament to their glory days, proof that they had indeed happened and weren't part of some weird dream. Besides which, having his picture reminded her that she was friends with such a great guy and he wasn't another spectre from that dream. Frank was very real, he made her life complete. April liked Frank a lot more than she had ever told him. She couldn't tell him, no matter how much she wanted to. What if he laughed in her face. Who would she turn to then when she needed someone to talk to, someone to confide in, someone to be with, somebody to share her deepest thoughts with. They did seem to share their thoughts, even without speaking. She had never found anybody she connected so deeply with. They were two sides of the same coin. But she knew Frank, knew him well enough to know that he didn't feel the same way, if he did he would have said something by now. Men are supposed to be the ones to ask, aren't they? Frank had had long enough to ask and he hadn't. Hadn't even hinted at it. So Ipso Facto he didn't feel the same way about her. Stands to reason, she thought.

A single tear squeezed its way out of the corner of her eye. It landed on the back of her remaining hand. When most people cry they reach for the tissues and wipe their eyes dry. When April cried she reached for the notebook and wrote until all the bad feelings were out on paper. This was one of those times, she felt bad enough to write a whole novel in one sitting. Her handwriting was bad, no, worse than bad, it was nearly illegible. Frank often said, when reading her writing, that the people breaking the Enigma code had an easier time than he did. It wasn't because she was stupid, she had a degree after all, it wasn't that she wrote too fast, she wasn't dyslexic and didn't have any other condition that she knew of. No, it was much worse than that. Her writing hand had been brutally severed, even after all this time she was still getting used to it.

This particular piece of writing took the form of a letter. A letter to Frank, detailing all her inner most hopes and dreams. But sadly Frank would never receive this letter. As she would never send it.

III – Frank (Yesterday)

Frank was sat in his chair beside a park bench. She was over by the burger stand getting them some hotdogs and cans of coke. He'd offered to help her bring the food back, but she'd argued that she could quite easily do it. If she'd had both her arms she would happily have accepted his offer. But because she only had one, she felt she had to prove herself at every available opportunity. Frank understood how she felt, when he'd still had his legs he never understood why disabled people looked angry when he offered to help. He hated being reminded that he was different. That's part of the reason he liked April so much, she didn't make him feel like an outsider, like society's unwanted son. She made him feel right at home, like he belonged.

Frank turned to look for her. There was quite a crowd gathering round the burger stand. He didn't have very good eyesight but he could pick her out easily enough. He could tell by the way she moved, the way her hair swayed. She had sensed him looking and turned round, he couldn't see but he knew she was smiling. She went to wave with the missing arm, she looked at it briefly and then waved with the other arm. Frank waved back, smiling broadly. She would be coming back soon and he still hadn't thought of anything to say. He massaged his temples with his index fingers, he desperately needed to come up with something, anything really. It's just that if he didn't think of something to say it would just burst out.

"I love you," he said under his breath, he was still rubbing at his head.

"What was that Frank?" April said softly from behind him.

"What… oh, nothing."

"You don't look too good, are you feeling ok?" she asked with genuine concern.

"Fine, I've just got a bit of a headache, that's all," he lied. She began to root through her bag for the tub of paracetamol she carried.

"I can't ever remember you having a serious headache since we met," a more serious note crept into her voice, "you remember that day Frank?"

"I've been trying to forget!" Frank shouted without meaning to. There it was. Out in the open. He hadn't meant that he regretted meeting her, but that's how she'd taken it.

IV – April (Yesterday)

April always enjoyed her trips to the park. Especially when Frank came. No matter how she'd felt before, she was always in a good mood when she'd seen him. It had been her idea to feed the ducks, she'd told him about one of her earliest memories. She'd been with her grandmother years before, in the same park, on the same bench. The memories had come back while she threw the bread; happiness and nostalgia mixed into one neat little bundle. That's when April suggested that she go get some hotdogs. She wasn't hungry, she was just afraid that she'd start crying if she didn't do something. That wasn't going to happen, Frank wasn't going to see her acting like a fool. That's why she'd snapped at him when he offered to help. His face had drawn in on itself and she instantly regretted it. He'd only had good intentions and she'd shouted at him for it.

April realised she was at the front of the queue and ordered the food. A bird had landed on the top of the burger stand, it had a badly torn wing. It was a pure white dove with shiny eyes. Another one joined it. This one had mangled feet and hobbled painfully when it landed. They began to sing together in perfect harmony. Her heart went out to them. Regardless of their injuries, they were the most majestic creatures she had ever seen. That's when she made up her mind, to do something about these feelings she'd had for so long. To just bite the bullet and tell him everything. April felt eyes on her, Frank's eyes. She turned to face them, hearing the flapping of wings behind her as the birds departed. He was still there where she had left him. A smile spread on her face, she started waving. Her face reddened when she realised which hand she was waving with. She waved with the other, hoping he hadn't noticed.

"Hey Miss, do you want any sauce with these?"

"One plain, mustard on the other please," she said, as she turned back to the vendor.

April walked back towards Frank. He was facing away, looking into the pond. As she got closer she saw that he was slumped forward in his chair, rubbing at his temples. April wondered if now was the right time to be telling him how she felt. He didn't look very good. She told him as much while putting the hotdogs down on the bench. Plain one for her. Mustard for him. That's the way it'd always been. What he said next shocked her.

"I've been trying to forget!"

Moments ago, she was sure she had loved him, now his callousness had brought tears to her eyes and doubt to her mind.

"Bastard!" she cried, running off into the park. Frank would have chased her but he wasn't strong enough to move his chair at the speed she had been running.

V – Frank (Seven Years Ago)

The sun was shining and not a cloud dotted the blue sky. Here he was, wearing trousers on such a scorcher of a day. Normally, he'd have worn shorts and shown off his legs, they weren't award winners but he had noticed the more than occasional approving glance from the female students. But today he couldn't afford to, today he had an interview. He hadn't got his degree yet but he had good reports to back him up and the job was being aimed specifically at students.

He was hot already and he'd only walked about fifty yards. When Frank reached the road he saw that a taxi was just cruising past. Lucky me, he thought waving the taxi down. The taxi pulled over to his side of the road and stopped. Frank clambered in the back seat and reached back to close the door. A hand held it open. He looked around and what he saw took his breath away. An amazingly pretty girl with long, blonde hair tied behind her head.

"Mind if we share?" she said, with a soft voice.

VI – April (Seven Years Ago)

The sun was magnificent, it shone as if to make up for the previous three months of greydom it had inflicted upon them. It was the sort of day made to have poems written about, April made a mental note to do just that.

She had a creative writing class today so she could do just that. First things first though, she had to get to the university somehow. She hadn't been here long and hadn't gotten used to the route yet. Then that cute guy walked out from D block. April's heart leapt, she'd seen him a few times before. It wasn't even as if he was that good looking, it was just something about the way he moved. It spoke of gentleness and quiet confidence. The guy didn't appear to know that April was watching so she carried on. All too soon he reached the end of the road, her heart sank. She had an idea though, she'd ask him for directions. That's when he got into a taxi and her heart sank even lower. She stopped for a moment and then, without thinking, she grabbed the door as he closed it.

"Mind if we share?" she said, her voice sounding stupid in her own ears.

VII – Frank and April (Seven Years Ago)

"Mind if we share?"

It hung between them for a few seconds while they looked into each other's eyes.

"No," Frank said flatly, the struggle to keep his voice even had rendered it emotionless, robotic. Her face dropped and she began to close the door. "Hey, I meant no I don't mind not no you can't."

She smiled and got in while he shuffled over behind the driver.

"Thank you," she said.

204

"You're welcome," he replied, meaning it.

They were silent again and he said something just so he could hear her voice again. "Which halls are you in?"

"South Village."

"Seriously, same here, which block are you in?" Frank was genuinely interested.

"E block, over by the car park, how about you?" she asked, even though she knew the answer.

"I'm in D, how come I've never seen you before?"

"Maybe you have and didn't know it," she said, trying to hide her growing excitement.

"No, I don't think so, I'd have remembered," he smiled. She giggled despite herself.

That's when the driver interrupted them.

"Don't mind lovebirds, but in two seconds this meter's going on whether you've told me where you're going or not!"

From the set of his jaw April could see the guy wasn't going to say the destination, although he would tell the driver where to go. She reached out and touched his hand, he turned to her and the angry look softened until it became a smile.

"The St. Charles building," they said at the same time and laughed.

They were both very aware of the time they were wasting with small talk. One of them would have to take the plunge and ask the other the important question or the taxi ride would be the end of it.

"I'm sorry, I never caught your name," she said, holding out her hand. "I'm April."

"I'm Frank, pleased to meet you." He took her hand then stopped, he wasn't sure what to do next. Do you shake a lady's hand or kiss it? After a few moments of indecision, he just held it, relishing the warmth of their touch. Electricity.

"How come you're in E block then, I thought that was just for first year students?" he asked.

"Well… I am a first year," she answered plainly.

"Oh, I had you pegged as a second maybe even a third year student." His surprise was obvious.

"Why, do I look old?" she joked.

"No, nothing like that. It's just first years generally walk around with shocked, wide eyed expressions." While he talked, he pulled the face he was describing and bobbed his mouth like a goldfish. Again they both laughed. It was the laugh of close friends, or lovers.

Their laughter was silenced by the squeal of brakes. They looked to the front and saw an over turned truck. It was growing larger in the windscreen. They all realised they weren't going to have time to stop. They all realised they weren't going to have time to scream. The sound of crunching metal and smashing glass silenced them. Frank's last act was to throw himself between April and the onrushing wall of jagged metal.

The Legend Of Cloth Face
by Chris Page aged 14

My best friend, Harry, is dead.

I killed him.

My girlfriend, Aurora, is lying in a hospital bed suffering from two bullet wounds in the stomach.

I fired those bullets.

My name is Cloth-Face and I am damned to live in a world of sorrow and loss. I have two lives and I am despised by other humans in both; hated, shunned and utterly lost.

It didn't used to be like this. Just a few millennium-like months ago, I was normal. Just a few months ago, I discovered my true self. Just a few months ago, the old me died.

Before I became Cloth-Face my name was... Killian, Killian Christopher Swift. I lived... in a city that I cannot name, a city I don't want to name... a city I hate, New York.

Why do I hate New York? I have given everything to that city and yet it has given me nothing but sorrow. I have tried my hardest to help its people. I have fought those who have done malice against it.... and yet they hate me?

Why?

I sit on the high point of a skyscraper, wishing I could find the truth...

I am Cloth-Face. I use my equipment as well as I can.

207

My main weapon is my Jo Staff and my ice pick, that doubles up as a hook blaster, allowing me to scale the buildings of New York. My two IMI Desert Eagle automatic pistols, my primary means of long range combat. Then there's my mask, made from the cloth that gives me my name. I am armed… I am ready… I want revenge. I want to find the man who made me shoot Harry and Aurora by accident. I want to avenge my only friends. I know who he is, I know where he is, I know how to kill him.

His name is Isaac T. Rainer. He is fifty three years old, five feet and ten inches tall. To almost everyone in the world he is a hero, a multibillionaire, a business and economical tycoon, a family man who donates millions of dollars to charity each fiscal year. He's the kind of guy mothers want their kids to grow up to be like, fathers want to aspire to. He's a childhood hero. Yeah, right.

What if I were to tell you that Isaac T. Rainer, living saint, was in fact Grendel. Yeah, hard to believe isn't it. I didn't believe it when I found out. A great man, a man who seems to care about every world issue from abortion to racism, couldn't possibly be Grendel, head of the S.E.R.P.E.N.T. organisation, the largest organised crime section in the world. Al Qaeda, the Mafia, the Triads? Don't make me laugh. Those guys are the equivalent of kids who think that nicking Mars bars from the local 7-11 is daring and clever compared to S.E.R.P.E.N.T.

I know what you want to know, why did Grendel and S.E.R.P.E.N.T. get a fix on my family, out of the millions of families everywhere? Why destroy my life when he could have destroyed thousands and millions of others?

Long story.

It all started a few years back. My grandfather, Shaun, was a reporter for the New York Times. He helped me get a job, back in 2005, when I needed it. My grandfather was a brilliant reporter, always out to get the story, always ready to do what it took to get the truth. He was certain that Grendel was someone high up in New York society and he made it his mission in life to find out who it was. Of course, I helped him. If I had known what would happen back then, I would have stopped him, burned all his work… but I can't change the past.

My grandfather and I gathered mounds of evidence; bank statements, documents, computer files… everything we thought we would need to incriminate Rainer. We even got an interview with him. We thought we were so clever, taking in every move he made, every time a muscle twitched in his temple when we asked him a difficult question. We were foolish, naïve; we thought that Rainer would never guess we were onto him. It would be the story of the decade.

Yet we were wrong, so very wrong. Rainer knew exactly what we had planned. He let us imagine that we were safe and that nothing could go wrong. Then, when we least expected it, he struck.

It happened on a Saturday in April. It was a beautiful day and I was helping my grandfather and grandmother do their shopping. We packed bulging plastic bags into my grandfather's battered Mustang, when my grandpa remembered that we'd forgotten printer paper. I went back in the store to get it. I should have died that day. In a way the printer paper saved my life. I walked into the shop... and then was knocked flat by a blast wave that seared my skin. I was slammed to the floor and lay dazed. I could hear screams and shouts and burning, the crackling of burning, but all so far away.

While we had been shopping, S.E.R.P.E.N.T. agents planted a small yield car bomb under my grandpa's rusty motor. The explosion killed my grandfather instantly and blinded my grandmother. I was knocked out, but alive.

I knew it was Rainer. Who else would want to kill us? But no one would believe me. Isaac Rainer? A killer? Rubbish! How dare you even suggest such a great man could kill your grandfather! No one would believe me. Who would care if the grandfather of an Irish reporter had been murdered by Isaac Rainer.

For the first six months after my grandfather's death I saw no-one, not my best friend Harry, nor my girlfriend Aurora. I dedicated myself to rigorous physical and mental training. I taught myself to fight, to kill men with my bare hands. I mastered a style of fighting using twin Desert Eagle handguns, wielding them with lethal accuracy. I taught myself to be faster, stronger, smarter than any other man. I would seek vengeance, I would bring justice to those who thought they were above the law and I would help the ordinary people. Cloth-Face was born.

For the first year I was a legend. I attacked S.E.R.P.E.N.T. activities, I brought their people to justice, I saved the lives of those they threatened. The people of New York even called me the "Guardian Angel". In twelve months I had brought S.E.R.P.E.N.T. to its knees… but my wave of glory was not to last. I should have known that. I was a fool.

Then things went so very horribly wrong. I don't know how, but Grendal aka Rainer found out who I was. He had the edge in our war because he could now attack the ones I loved. And he did. He employed Jean L'Rouge, a top French killer, to do his dirty work. L'Rouge was brutal. He tricked me into shooting my best friend, Harry. Then he took my girlfriend hostage. When I went to save her, he used her as a human shield to protect himself from my bullets. Then he left me.

He's dead now. I tracked him down and shot him myself. In his dying moments he told me how to get past Grendel's security. Maybe he thought that info would save his life. It didn't.

So now, here I am, atop the Empire State building,

looking down over the city of Manhattan, spread out below me like a map. I used to come here often to admire the view and feel the power of looking down on the millions of people far below me. No feeling of power, of joy, of hope, not now. Only hate and vengeance. My mask felt tight against my face, my fingers inadvertently stroking the butts of my D-eagles. I know what I have to do.

I wrapped my cloak around my shoulders, pulled down my cloth mask and covered my face. I fired the piton from my axe into a gargoyle, made sure that it was secure and gripped the axe handle.

Grendel… you killed Harry, you made me shoot Aurora, now you must pray that I never find you.

Cloth-Face has returned.

The Pied Piper – With A Twist
by Caitlin Curtis aged 12

It's strange. However many times I tell the story of what happened to me that Sunday, however much detail I use and however many facts I include, no-one believes me. They just laugh and tell me I've got a wild imagination. Ha. That's rich. Wild.

My story starts in the sleepy village of Whistlewillow, the village next to my home town. It's normally a very peaceful place, always calm and warm with a happy atmosphere. But despite the almost perfect location, not many people go there.

Well, except on the 1st July. That's the day when the famous Whistlewillow Market opens.

I love Whistlewillow Market. It's filled with brightly coloured stalls, all displaying some type of delicious food from all over the world. I can remember mouth-watering Dutch cakes, creamy Belgian chocolate and the sizzling pancakes which were so amazingly gorgeous I ate ten. There was even a stall that sold crystals and emeralds and other sparkling jewels that glittered when they caught the sun (and just to bring us all back down to earth – good old English pie and peas). I really wanted to go again. I pestered my Mum until she finally agreed to let me. What's more, I was allowed to go on my own. When the day came, I was so excited I was surprised you couldn't see my heart jumping through my ribs. Little did I know, this time, my visit wouldn't be as peaceful as the last.

I arrived at the market at 12.00 noon exactly. I wasn't the only person there. Hundreds of people had gathered just to spend a day there. The roads were so busy you couldn't even see the tarmac. All you saw was a line of cars, one after the other, winding through the village and over the green hills beyond.

The Whistlewillow Market was as good as I remembered. In fact, it was even better. I was very happy, surrounded by chocolate and cakes and all the other things I love. I managed to eat eleven pancakes this time, but sadly only one bowl of pie and peas. I could hear the happy shouts of the people around me, and the villagers' yells exclaiming things like the cakes were half price and the pie was only 99p. I finally settled down on a dark wooden bench with my Raspberry Ripple ice cream, in the shade of a massive truck, felling very happy as I licked away.

It was such a hot day, I felt as though I was walking around with my head on fire. The sun was beaming down on us all, bouncing off car windows as though it was in a room full of mirrors. Wherever I looked, I had to shield my eyes from the blinding light. Luckily, I was in the shadow of a huge truck. This particular huge truck had a lot to do with the story.

On the side of the truck was a giant poster – it said 'Mungo's Travelling Animal Circus'. It took me a few seconds to realise that this truck was the travelling circus. And it was filled with performing animals. By the sound of it, these animals weren't very happy. They had obviously travelled a long way in the sweltering heat and had had enough. I could hear them ferociously banging on the sides of the truck, wanting to escape. And that's exactly what they did. Escape.

With one colossal shove from an oversized elephant, the truck door crashed to the floor with a loud bang. I jumped so high with shock I got half of my ice cream all over my face. The animals all poured out of the truck – elephants, lions, cheetahs, monkeys, hyenas, giraffes, hippos – too many to count. A stampede of rushing animals, all loose in Whistlewillow Market.

Chaos broke out immediately. People fled in all directions, being chased by lions. Screams filled the air as everyone tried to escape the usually quiet town. Everyone leapt from their cars just in time – before elephants crushed them beneath their huge feet, as easily as we would crush leaves. Cheetahs and hyenas were having races from the chocolate stall to the pancake booth (the cheetahs won). A large hippo had fallen asleep in the middle of the road, causing even more traffic jams. The monkeys were raiding the local pub, stealing rum and whisky and getting very drunk, tying innocent bystanders to lampposts with bunting from the pork pie stall.

I froze with horror as the village before me went from a nice peaceful place to one of total havoc and destruction. I was too surprised and shocked, I didn't even think of running until I heard a low snarl behind me.

Slowly turning round, I found myself face to face with a huge lion with a thick brown mane hanging around his face, his teeth bared looking very large and white. My heart was beating furiously with fear and I seemed to have stopped breathing. I told myself to keep calm. My eyes scanned the area around me looking for a way I could escape.

The lion moved closer. It was now so near to me that I could feel its hot rumbling breath, so near in fact that I could just reach out and touch it. Although I really couldn't see why I would want to touch a great, snarling lion. The lion moved closer. Then it suddenly opened his huge mouth, leant towards me and – licked my nose! It wasn't a pleasant experience but it was certainly better than being devoured by a lion. I sighed with relief. The lion continued to lick my nose. No, it wasn't my nose, it was the ice cream the lion was licking. A lion who liked ice cream?

I turned around. A monkey was perched on a rock with a bottle of rum in his hand. He then licked my hand which was also covered in ice cream. I realised all of the circus animals must like ice cream. That one thought developed into a brilliant plan.

I ran forward to where I remembered the ice cream stall was. The owner of the stall was cornered by a hyperactive hyena. The hyena froze as soon as I came near and began licking my arm, desperate to get the ice cream.

"Can I borrow some ice cream?" I said politely, as if I hadn't noticed animals running around the village.

"How can you think about ice cream at a time like this?!" screeched the owner, but I had already picked up a tub of Raspberry Ripple and was walking away.

I poured the whole contents of the tub over my head, shivering as the cold substance tickled down my back.

Vincent Buxton
2005.

217

Then I began to run around the village with a trail of animals behind me.

More and more animals joined the line. Soon the whole circus was following me, including the hippo which had fallen asleep earlier. The animals were trailing after me as if they were hypnotised. I was like the Pied Piper of Hamelin, with a twist.

All the villagers were staring at me as in amazement. I remember them looking with wonder and admiration in their eyes. I kept all the animals under control until the RSPCA came and then all the animals were taken away to the zoo where they would be fed on ice cream. (I later found out why the animals loved Raspberry Ripple ice cream. It was the treat that the circus used to persuade the animals to do tricks!) The village of Whistlewillow was saved. All thanks to me!

The trouble is, no-one believes me. Whenever I tell them how I saved the Whistlewillow Market from wild circus animals, they just laugh at me and say, "What? How can animals like ice cream? How can monkeys drink rum? How can all this happen? How can a child save the day?" Well, I did, and that's how. Now the big question...

Do you believe me?

The Foster Home
by Hayden Larder aged 14

"Just follow me upstairs dear and I'll show you where to put your stuff."

The eccentric old lady smelled of lavender. This is weird, I thought, a bungalow with six floors!!

As I climbed the stairs, the loud chiming of a grandfather clock made me jump. Along the walls there were loads of strange paintings. One of them was a red and purple striped horse. It stared at me with evil eyes.

"Here we are," said the old lady, beckoning me into a dark room, "try not to worry about your mum, sweetheart."

"I'm not your sweetheart, I'm Amiee. My Mum's the only one who's allowed to call me sweetheart, only she doesn't call me anything anymore. All she does is lie in a hospital bed with a grey face."

"Unpack your stuff, dearie, and then come down for tea."

As the old lady walked out of the room, I wondered what can of horrible muck she would give me to eat.

It didn't take long to unpack my binbag. It made me feel like rubbish having my clothes in a black plastic bag. That social worker who came to collect me should have given me a proper bag. Stupid cow.

When I looked around the room there were loads of strange things. In the corner there was a didgeridoo, on the dressing table there was an antique globe and a pair of glistening glasses. This woman is a right weirdo.

Suddenly I felt very tired. I sat down on the old rusty bed. It bounded up as I sank back. Something wet splashed on my hand and I realised I was crying. I knew my mum might never come out of hospital. How would I stand living here in this awful place? How will I stand not having my mum to cuddle me?

"Alright love? Tea's ready."

A horrible smell seeped upstairs. It was a mixture of greasy meat and sprouts. I wondered if anyone had bothered to tell here I am veggie.

"Come on darling."

I trudged slowly downstairs, even though the smell was making me feel sick. On the table was a vegetable pie that looked home made. I tried a bit off my plate. To my surprise, it was gorgeous!! Since my mum has been ill, I haven't had any proper dinners. The old lady passed me a bubbling effervescent drink. I was starving. I started shovelling the food down fast.

"Slow down dearie, you'll choke."

I still didn't feel like talking to her but gave her a small smile.

"Tomorrow is Sunday. We'll go to church and pray for your mum."

God can't cure terminal cancer, I thought. I hardly slept that night, the bed was creaky and my eyes were itchy. Just as I was drifting off, the old woman crept in and said, "Up you get lovie, we are going to light a candle for your poor mother." I realised it was morning.

The old woman made me some delicious porridge with honey. I'd never been so hungry.

At the church, the old woman pressed 50p into my hand and told me to go and buy a candle.

"Here, I'll light it for you," she said.

That's when I made the wish, "Mum, please don't die." But it was too late.

I heard my mum whispering to me. "I'll never forget you Amiee." My heart squeezed too tight.

The Lighthouse
by John Gay aged 13

There was a little town called Hook Coast. It was a nice little town with lots of small shops and one or two pubs. It had a dock with a few fishing boats and a big lighthouse. The people were kind and generous. Most of the men were fishermen at the docks.

The lighthouse keeper was a bit secretive, but everyone knew his naughty son called Bill. Bill sometimes turned the big light off so boats would crash and his dad would turn it back on.

One day Bill turned the light off, but his dad didn't come up so he went to look for him. He found him on the floor. Dead. Bill started crying and then he heard a huge explosion outside. He ran outside and he saw boat after boat crashing in the dock. He ran up to the top of the lighthouse, turned the light on and jumped off.

Ghostly Visions
by Benjamin Hopkins aged 12

My friend Jack arranged to meet me for the weekend at a cabin he just bought in an area of the county I had never been to before. This was to be a stress-free weekend away from the bustling city life we were used to. I'm looking forward to the break as this is a new experience for me. The cabin is located way up in the mountains, a bit too far from civilisation for my liking but I wouldn't be put off by this.

Driving up the long and winding road on the Friday night, I became a bit apprehensive as there were no lights, and the leafless, withered trees gave a very eery setting. As I continued on, I had the growing feeling that things were not as they should be. I don't know why I felt this but I guess you could call it sixth sense or something. As I drove on, I finally came upon the cabin...

My friend boasted what a fantastic place this was. When I finally pulled up to the cabin, I thought I glimpsed shadowy figures out of the corner of my eye. I put this down to tiredness, but I still felt a bit uneasy.

There wasn't much lighting around the cabin and I felt very alone and a bit hesitant about getting out of my car. Why I should feel this way I don't know. There were some lights on in the cabin so I knew I didn't have anything to worry about.

As I got out of the car, I retrieved my overnight bag from the back seat and made my way to the front door. It was very quiet except I thought I could hear voices in the trees around me. Nonsense, I thought. There wasn't anyone around for miles, except for my friend Jack and he was inside the cabin, no doubt cooking a fantastic dinner for us, or so I was hoping!

I knocked loudly on the door. No answer. I knocked again, louder, but again, no answer. I proceeded to walk around the house to see if I could see in the windows for my friend. Perhaps he was napping and couldn't hear my knocking.

As I made my way around the house, looking through the windows, Jack wasn't anywhere to be seen. Becoming concerned, I rang his number from my mobile phone. The phone was answered but it wasn't Jack, or I didn't think it was Jack. There was a high pitched scream at the end of the phone and I didn't know what to think, could it be that something was wrong with the reception or was Jack in some kind of trouble?

Making my way around to the front of the cabin, I tried the door and to my surprise it was unlocked. I walked into the foyer, dropping my bag, and made my way hesitantly through the cabin. The cabin was large with rustic furniture and seemed a bit menacing. Not as welcoming as I thought it would be. Seeing no sign of Jack, I began to call out his name. Nothing, no reply at all. At this point I became very worried and wanted to run from the cabin.

I wanted to be out of the cabin and into my car as quickly

as I could. When I stepped out the front door, I could hear someone calling my name. It sounded like Jack. I turned my attention to the path that was cut through the trees. I could still hear Jack calling to me and felt relieved; I guess he heard me knocking on his door whilst he was in the woods collecting firewood or something.

As I made my way down the path again, I thought I could see ghostly figures out of the corner of my eye. I began walking faster towards the direction I could hear Jack calling to me. I started to shout to Jack and he said he was coming. As I continued on there was no sight of Jack but I could still hear him calling to me. I carried on and on for what seemed like ages.

I came to a clearing and there was no sign of Jack and I became extremely frightened. I could hear voices whispering to me again. I became petrified with fear. I was running in circles and couldn't find my way. Jack, Jack. Help me! Where are you?!

Jack suddenly appeared out of nowhere and I was grateful to see him as I was terrified. I ran up to Jack and thought he looked dreadful and couldn't understand why as he knew I was coming to stay with him. I asked Jack what was wrong and he pointed to something in the trees. Out of the shadows came ghost-like figures. Again, I couldn't believe what I was seeing but they kept coming towards me and Jack. I turned around towards Jack but he was gone, just as if he had never been there.

I feared for my life as the figures approached me. I began to run but I had no idea where I was running. As the ghostly figures descended upon me, I cried again for Jack and he suddenly appeared as if by magic.

He quickly whispered to me to run down the path to my right and to keep going until I got to my car and not to stop for anything until I was well away from the cabin.

I ran for my life down the path and through the trees. I could see the ghostly figures around me but kept praying they would go away. I ran and ran and thought it was no good until I came upon the cabin and my car. I got into my car as quickly as I could and drove away even quicker and never looked back.

When I arrived home, I was in shock and couldn't get to grips with what I had just been through. Had I been dreaming it all? When I got into my house I called Jack's mobile number again but there was no answer. I was so exhausted that I just collapsed into bed.

The next morning I rang Jack's mobile and, when he answered, he reminded me he was in France skiing with his girlfriend. I was shaking and totally confused by this. I asked him if he had been at the new cabin and he didn't know what I was talking about. He asked if I was feeling okay and I said, yeah, and that I was sorry to bother him and that I must have been confused.

As I made my way to the bathroom I nearly tripped over my overnight bag which was fully packed. Why was it there and how did it get there …..?

The House Of Hell
by James Burlison aged 11

This story isn't like one of those stories where it's all nicey nicey and all the good people come through okay and the evil people die, oh no. The story I am about to tell you will make you realise that not all stories have a happy ending.

Crrreak! Went the front door of the house. Inside, the porch was dark and gloomy. The cool, dusty air stung Peter's eyes as he peered into the gloom, he wasn't looking forward to living in this ancient house at all. In fact, he wished they had never moved out of their cosy little cottage in Yorkshire in the first place.

"Well, it looks like this place hasn't had a spring clean in years!" said his mum disapprovingly, breaking the silence like a brittle twig.

"Yes dear," groaned Peter's dad resentfully as they entered the house. The door shut with a snap behind them as they pulled off their shoes and shrugged off their anoraks. Peter was already disliking the house greatly and by the look on his dad's sullen face, so was he. The rest of the week was devoted to his mum's incessant cleaning. Peter noticed something strange about this, no matter how much she vacuumed, dusted and polished, the house stayed as dark, dusty and dank as it was when they first arrived. This puzzled him greatly. However, this only redoubled her effort to get the house ship-shape and tidy and she was now constantly popping up here and there with a duster, polishing everything in sight.

Nine weeks passed before she finally gave up on cleaning the house and instead she began buying ornaments and crockery to put in all the rooms that, to her, looked messy. All except the attic, as the door to it was locked and would not open. Peter often heard strange unearthly noises coming from the attic and, every time he heard it, it sent shivers crawling up his spine. His mum insisted that it was just the pipes groaning and that he was being a big baby, fussing over nothing, but he knew it wasn't the pipes, it sounded very different to that. It sounded more like the screeching yell of thousands of demented rats being tortured with knives.

"Well at least nothing bad has happened," Peter thought to himself that night. Little did he know that the next day was to change all that in a terrible and horrifying way.

The next day there was a strange chill in the house and Peter knew something was amiss. His mum twittered on about heating failures and poor quality plumbing, as he ate his breakfast and did his teeth. Later on, he went into the kitchen where one of the tiles was glowing brightly, he approached it cautiously, reached out and touched it. Suddenly, it sank into the wall, scraping and sliding as it went. Silence. Peter was about to go and tell his parents, when the whole wall creaked noisily and slid out of sight. He turned around and headed straight for the chamber, as though he was being drawn to it by some powerful force. In the middle of the chamber was a small platform with a key on it. Peter picked it up. Set in the handle of the key was a strange black gem that glowed slightly. Suddenly, the wall began to slide back into place. Peter dived through the ever closing gap and landed flat on his face on the kitchen floor. The wall shut behind him with a dull thud, he ran to the living room to tell his dad what had happened. As he opened the door the smell of blood washed over him making him cough and splutter. In the corner, impaled on razor sharp spikes, was his dad! Peter ran over to him and saw a blood stained piece of paper stuck on one of the spikes with a message on it saying, "If you unlock the attic with the key of darkness then you will suffer the same fate as your father!" Then, as soon as he had seen it, it vanished into thin air, taking the smell with it too! "That's it," Peter thought. "I'm going to find out what's in the attic once and for all!"

That night, Peter crept up the rickety stairs to the attic, as quiet as a mouse. He hardly dared even breathe in case the thing in the attic heard him. He reached the top of the stairs after what seemed an age of slowly sneaking up the stairs. He fumbled with the key as he slid it into the lock. Slowly, he turned the key in the lock. Click! went the lock as the door creaked open.

Inside, it was as cold as a freezer and as dark as a black hole. He tiptoed across the dust thick floor, gazing all around him. Without realising where he was going, he walked straight into a pile of boxes. The boxes toppled over revealing a pile of skeletons with all the meat picked clean off them! Shaking from head to foot, he backed away, still looking at the pile of skeletons with utmost horror. Then, out of the gloom, leaped a giant spider about nine foot tall and ten foot wide. Peter screamed a scream loud enough to wake the dead, as the spider scuttled towards him faster than he could run, forcing him back into a corner. He was trapped! The spider knew this and began advancing menacingly with its jaws wide open until they were centimetres away from his face! Peter closed his eyes, waiting to feel the immense pain of his skull being crushed like an eggshell...

Acknowledgements

Our thanks go to

the children, whose tremendous efforts have made this possible.

all the schools whose collective help enabled us to co-ordinate this collection.

Liz, Helen and David for taking time out of their busy schedules to select future professional authors (perhaps!).

our illustrators, Vincent and Andrew, for adding that extra special something.

Dave for helping to bring it all together.

Mike for a title... which helps!

And, on a personal note, thank you Martin for the idea in the first place and, together with Rick, your patience and the occasional raised eyebrow!

Printed in the United Kingdom
by Lightning Source UK Ltd.
107300UKS00001B/7-60